A Horse for Jackie

Linda peered inside Copper's stall. Jackie stood by the mare's neck, the bridle hanging upside down in her hands.

"Uh . . . Jackie," Linda said quietly, "you're holding that wrong."

Jackie jumped, and the bridle fell to the straw. "I—I don't use this kind," she stammered.

Just then, Kathy led her horse up. "What's taking you guys so long?" she asked. "We're ready to hit the trail."

Quickly, Jackie bent to pick up the bridle, her face bright red.

"Why don't you count me out?" she said loudly. "Look, I don't know how to ride. I—I've never been on a horse in my entire life!"

Books in The Linda Craig Adventures series:

Available from MINSTREL Books

THE LINDA CRAIG ADVENTURES #7

A HORSE FOR JACKIE

By Ann Sheldon

A MINSTREL® BOOK

PUBLISHED BY POCKET BOOKS

New York   London   Toronto   Sydney   Tokyo

A MINSTREL PAPERBACK *ORIGINAL*

A Minstrel Book published by
POCKET BOOKS, a division of Simon & Schuster Inc.
1230 Avenue of the Americas, New York, NY 10020

Copyright © 1989 by Simon & Schuster Inc.
Cover artwork copyright © 1989 by Susan Tang
Produced by Mega-Books of New York, Inc.

ISBN: 0-671-67471-4

First Minstrel Books printing May 1989

10 9 8 7 6 5 4 3 2 1

THE LINDA CRAIG ADVENTURES is a trademark
of Simon & Schuster Inc.

LINDA CRAIG, A MINSTREL BOOK and colophon are
registered trademarks of Simon & Schuster Inc.

Printed in the U.S.A.

A HORSE FOR JACKIE

1 ♦♦♦♦

"This is going to be the best stunt the talent show has *ever* seen." Linda Craig rode her golden palomino, Amber, in big circles around the edge of the paddock at Rancho del Sol. In the middle of the paddock was Linda's best friend, Kathy Hamilton, sitting on her brown-and-white pinto, Patches. Both Kathy and her horse were watching nervously as Linda came closer.

"Are you sure you want to try this?" Kathy asked. "There are still three weeks before the show. You could come up with something else."

Lockwood's annual talent show was one of the highlights of the town's year. People came from miles around, dreaming up all sorts of acts and stunts. Since Linda loved horses, she had her act all worked out in her head.

"It's not *that* hard," she said to Kathy. "Just keep Patches still while I take a practice swing."

The idea was for Linda to swing from Amber's saddle onto Patches' back—right behind Kathy. When the talent show came around, Linda would be doing this with her friend Kelly Michaels. And they wouldn't be standing still—their horses would be cantering around in a circle.

But Kelly was older than Linda and worked Saturdays at the Flying Star Ranch. In return, Glen Manlon, who owned the ranch, boarded Kelly's horse, Cinder. Even though it was now late afternoon, Kelly would still be busy, so Kathy was standing in.

"Okay, get ready," Linda called. She tucked her long, dark hair behind her ears and brought Amber up beside Patches. This was the first time—but not the last—she would practice the swing over and over before trying the trick on a moving horse.

Dropping Amber's reins on the mare's neck, Linda kicked her feet free of the stirrups. She leaned over, clutched Kathy's left shoulder for support, and swung her right leg halfway across Patches' broad rump. "Almost there," she muttered.

Then Amber nickered and moved forward.

"Whoa!" Linda cried, but it was too late. The palomino had moved out from under her, and Linda was sliding down Patches' side. She grabbed for Kathy, nearly pulling her out of the saddle.

Kathy clung to her saddle pommel and began to laugh. "I don't think this is working out quite right," she said. "Hang on and pull yourself up behind me."

"That's what I'm trying to do," Linda puffed, kicking both legs as she tried to get a grip.

That's when Patches suddenly rounded his back and hopped sideways.

"Aaaaaaaaaaah!" Linda yelled as she bounced off the pinto's rump and fell to the dry grass below.

"Knock it off, Patches." Kathy reined her horse in and looked down at Linda. "Are you okay?"

"Except for a big dent in my pride, I think I'm all right." Linda got up and brushed off her jeans. "Thanks a lot, Patches."

"I guess he didn't like you hanging off his side like a sack of potatoes."

Linda had to grin. "Maybe he and Amber can come up with their own stunt. That was some trick Amber pulled. And no wonder," she said, pointing past the barn. "She was showing off for her friends Midnight and Shorty."

3

Kathy turned in the saddle. Amber was galloping toward two girls on horses. "Great," she said. "Amy and Marni are here."

Linda waved to the two red-haired girls. Amy and Marni Brown were sisters—Marni was Linda's age, twelve, and Amy was a year younger.

Earlier that week, Linda had invited a few of her friends to spend Saturday night at Rancho del Sol. She figured a slumber party would be the perfect place to try out their acts together.

Amber pranced around as the riders came into the paddock. Her white mane flew in the air, and her golden coat gleamed in the late-afternoon sun. Linda gave a shrill whistle. The sound stopped Amber in her tracks. She whirled around and with Shorty and Midnight not far behind, raced back toward Linda.

Linda grabbed her horse's dangling reins.

"Whoa!" she said sternly, then grinned, as the mare nuzzled her cheek with a velvety nose. Linda knew Amber hadn't ruined the trick on purpose. They both just needed a lot of practice.

"Hi," Marni said as she reined up her black Morgan horse, Midnight. Her sister was riding a calving pony, Shorty.

"Hi," Kathy and Linda both said. But Linda

4

blinked in confusion, looking back and forth between the two sisters.

"What did you do to your hair?" she asked. "You guys look like twins."

Usually, Amy's hair was poker straight. Now she fluffed it with her fingers. "I had it permed," she said. "It's for our act—you'll see," she added mysteriously.

"Wait till you see Linda's great trick," Kathy teased as they led their horses into the barn.

"We saw you falling off Patches," Amy said, looking puzzled. "Are you going to be a cowboy clown?"

"No." Linda gave her a look. "But if I don't get any better, Amber's going into the arena alone."

"That would probably suit this show-off just fine," Kathy said.

All the girls laughed. Amber wrinkled her lip and stuck her nose in the air as if she were laughing, too. Then she leaned over and nuzzled Linda, hoping for a piece of apple or carrot.

After the girls had bedded down the horses, they picked up their gear and headed for the ranch house.

"I wonder what's keeping Jackie," Linda said.

"Jackie?" Marni exclaimed. "You mean Jackie

Lee, the new kid in class—the one who's so stuck-up?"

"Why'd you invite *her?*" Kathy asked in an accusing tone.

"Oh, Jackie's not so bad," Linda protested. "I think she's just lonely."

"Well, she's sure going to *stay* lonely," Kathy grumbled, "especially if she keeps going around with her nose in the air."

"She's a snobby rich kid, is what I heard," Marni said. "Her dad bought Lucky Star Ranch. What a place! They say a movie star used to live there."

"Shhh. Here she comes." Linda pointed down the drive, where a girl with shoulder-length brown hair was walking toward them. She had a backpack slung over one shoulder and carried a guitar on a strap on the other. It had to be Jackie.

"Why don't you guys go on up to my room and stash your things? I'll wait for Jackie and meet you on the patio. And try to be nice," Linda added quickly as Jackie drew nearer.

"Yeah, okay," her friends replied as they filed into the spacious ranch house where Linda and her older brother, Bob, lived with their grandparents,

A Horse for Jackie

Bronco and Doña Mallory. Rancho del Sol had been the Craigs' home ever since their parents had died several years before.

Gravel crunched under Jackie's feet as she came closer, a shy smile of greeting on her face.

"I hope you didn't walk the whole way!" Linda joked, trying to put Jackie at ease.

"No, I, uh . . . I got dropped off."

"Well, glad you could make it. Everyone's on the patio. I hope you're hungry."

"Hungry? I could eat a horse," Jackie said enthusiastically. Then she clapped a hand to her mouth. "Sorry," she apologized. "I didn't mean—"

Laughing, Linda took Jackie's guitar and led her into the ranch house. "Don't worry about it. I'm pretty hungry, too."

Jackie followed her through the dining room and onto the flower-scented patio. The other girls, busy spooning spicy hamburger, cheese, and tomato into taco shells, waved.

"So where's your horse?" Marni asked. "We figured you'd ride over."

"Yeah, we all wanted to see that new Thoroughbred you told us about at school." Kathy set her taco on her plate and gave Jackie a cool look.

"Well . . ." Jackie hesitated, her tan face flushing pink. "My dad and I haven't bought it yet."

"Thoroughbreds are really beautiful," Linda said, trying to rescue Jackie. "And they sure run fast."

"You must be *some* rider to handle a Thoroughbred," Kathy added.

"Boy, does that taco look great!" Jackie exclaimed. She slid the backpack off her shoulder and grabbed a plate.

Luisa, the Mallorys' housekeeper, bustled onto the patio, carrying a pitcher.

"Anybody interested in fresh-squeezed limeade?" she asked.

"I am!" Linda held up her glass. As Luisa poured, Linda glanced at Jackie. The new girl had chosen a lawn chair away from the others. Linda hoped that inviting her hadn't been a mistake.

But the meal went smoothly enough, and after dinner, Amy and Marni ran through their skit.

"You have to pretend that there's a mirror right here," Marni told them, pointing to the middle of the patio. Then she faced Amy and raised her arm. Amy moved her arm in the exact same way. In perfect unison, the two sisters imitated each other's movements.

"The funny part comes when Marni goes to comb her hair, but in the mirror, I decide to scratch my head," Amy explained.

"We need some more ideas, so if anyone has a suggestion . . ." Marni added, looking around at the others stretched comfortably on the lounge chairs.

Linda patted her stomach. "I'm too full to think."

"What a lazybones," Marni said. "I bet if someone mentioned a moonlight ride, you'd jump at the chance."

Instantly, Linda sat bolt upright and yelled, "Good idea!" She sprang to her feet, and with a whoop, Kathy joined her.

Only Jackie stayed seated.

The new girl cleared her throat, and the others turned to look at her. "Too bad I don't have a horse," she said, a little too loudly. "Guess I'll have to wait here."

"Oh, come on, we've got lots of horses you can ride!" Linda pulled Jackie up off her chair.

"But I don't have any cowboy boots, either." Jackie stuck a foot into the air.

"So? Are you afraid of getting your sneakers dirty?" Kathy asked teasingly.

"No, but . . ." Jackie fumbled for an answer. "What if a horse steps on my toe?"

"Then you'll yell 'Ouch!' " Marni said. "Just like the rest of us would."

Laughing, the girls started down the path through Doña's garden and around the back of the ranch house. As they raced toward the barn, Linda glanced over her shoulder. Jackie was lagging behind. Linda figured she must be feeling bad because she didn't have a horse of her own. She slowed to let the new girl catch up.

"You can ride Copper Princess," she told Jackie. "She's not a fiery Thoroughbred, but I think you'll like her."

Jackie frowned in the moonlight. "Look, you don't have to bother," she insisted.

"It's no bother at all."

"Let's go, you guys!" Kathy called from inside the lighted barn.

"Coming!" Linda shouted.

"I don't—" Jackie protested, but Linda was on her way to the barn.

Jackie followed her to the tack room, where Linda handed her new friend a bridle.

"Try this on Copper," she said, pointing to a flaxen-maned chestnut horse quietly munching hay in one of the stalls. "Amber's in the stall next door, so holler when you've got it on, and I'll bring you a saddle."

Jackie nodded slowly, and Linda grabbed her own saddle and bridle. As soon as she opened the door, Amber lifted her head and nickered a greeting.

"No brushing tonight, girl," Linda said as she tossed the blanket and saddle on the mare's back. The palomino snorted in protest, then grabbed one last bite of hay before Linda popped the bit into her mouth and slid the headstall over her ears.

"How're you coming?" Linda called into Copper's stall. There was no answer.

Linda gave Amber's girth a tug, then led the mare from the stall. Copper's door was open, and Linda peered inside.

Jackie stood by the mare's neck, the bridle hanging upside down in her hands. She held the metal bit backward and was awkwardly pressing it against the horse's mouth.

"Uh, Jackie," Linda said quietly. "You're holding the bridle wrong."

Jackie jumped, and the bridle fell to the straw. "I—I don't use this kind," she stammered.

Just then, Kathy led her horse behind Amber.

"What's taking you guys so long?" she asked. "We're ready to hit the trail."

Quickly, Jackie bent to pick up the bridle, her face bright red.

"Why don't you count me out?" she said loudly. "Look, I don't know how to ride. I—I've never been on a horse in my entire life!"

2 ◆◆◆◆

"You can't ride?" Linda repeated in a puzzled voice.

"That's what I said!" Jackie replied defensively.

"But I thought you were supposed to be a hotshot rider," Kathy said accusingly.

"I never *said* I could ride." Jackie's voice got softer as she looked at the ground.

"Then what about that Thoroughbred we've all been hearing about?" Kathy went on.

Jackie stared down at the bridle still in her hands. "I made it all up," she admitted. "It's the horse I want, but . . ."

Linda could tell that Jackie was upset. She took the bridle from the other girl. "No big deal," Linda said with a smile. "We can teach you to ride in no time."

"Unless you don't want to," Kathy put in.

"Oh, but I do." Jackie's face brightened as she looked up at the other two girls.

Linda joined her in the stall. "Okay, let's start with lesson number one—How to Put on the Bridle."

Jackie looked at Linda gratefully. "I was afraid you guys wouldn't invite me if you knew I didn't ride," she admitted. "I mean, you've got your own horses and everything."

"Even so, sometimes we make mistakes and fall off." Kathy looked at Linda and laughed.

"Very funny." Linda untangled the bridle, then showed Jackie how to hold it.

"See, the bit goes in the left hand and the headstall in your right."

"Headstall?"

"That's the piece that goes over the ears," Linda explained.

Jackie bit her lip. "I feel so dumb."

"Oh, don't worry, bridling a horse is easy," Kathy said. "Unless it clamps its mouth shut or tosses its head in the air or spits the bit out."

Jackie frowned in confusion, and her shoulders slumped.

14

"Come on, Kathy," Linda protested. "You're getting her all mixed up. Why don't you join Amy and Marni. You know the trail. We'll catch up with you guys."

Kathy opened her mouth and gave Linda an I-thought-you-were-my-friend look. Then she clamped her lips shut, grabbed Patches' reins, and headed out of the barn. Halfway out, she looked over her shoulder. "Sure, we'll wait—but hurry."

When they were gone, Jackie sighed. "I'm just not doing anything right."

Linda laughed and shook her head. "You'd better get used to it. Around here, every girl thinks she's a riding instructor."

"Well, I don't think Kathy would call me a star pupil," Jackie groaned. "And how can I learn enough to go on the trail ride with you right now?"

"It's not that hard." Linda quickly bridled Copper Princess, then went to get a saddle. Loose in the aisle, Amber was visiting Rocket, Linda's brother's bay gelding. Amber's head hung over the stall door, and Linda could hear Rocket squeal.

Linda smiled at Jackie's worried look. "Here's the plan—I'll lead you next to Amber." She threw a striped blanket, then a heavy western saddle onto

Copper's back. "You'll be perfectly safe, sitting up there. And after tonight, you'll be able to say you finally rode a horse."

Ten minutes later, the two girls were riding down the trail. The flat countryside was bathed in moonlight, and a warm breeze rustled through the tall grass. Eager to catch up with the others, Amber pricked up her ears and began to prance.

"Whoa, girl." Linda stroked the mare's neck to calm her.

"Sorry to slow you down," Jackie said. Her hands were wrapped tight around the pommel of the western saddle, and she wore a determined frown on her face.

"No problem. I'm just glad you decided to come along. It's such a beautiful night!"

Jackie gave her a tight nod of agreement. Her shoulders were tense, and her legs clutched Copper's sides like a vise.

"Just relax and go with the movement of the horse," Linda told her. "If you feel yourself slipping, holler and I'll stop."

Up ahead, Linda spied a dark shape—it was Amy on Shorty. As they came closer, she heard the other girls' voices. They were talking about Jackie, but Linda couldn't quite make out the words. She hoped Jackie couldn't, either.

"Here we are, guys!" she called.

Amy turned and waved. Her face glowed in the moonlight.

When Linda and Jackie caught up to the others, Kathy put her fingers to her lips.

"Listen," she whispered.

A coyote howled in the distance. Then another barked a cry, answering the first.

"Neat, huh?" Marni said quietly.

"As long as they don't come too close," Jackie replied with a shudder.

A loud rustle in the bushes made her whip around in the saddle. "What was that?"

Linda laughed. "That's just Patches trying to bite off a branch. Kathy's horse will eat anything."

Jackie gave them a nervous smile. "It scared me for a second. You don't meet many coyotes in Los Angeles. Living in the city, all you have to worry about is cars and smog."

"Come on." Kathy waved them ahead. "We'd better get going, or it'll be midnight before we get back."

As they rode along the trail, the flutter of wings

17

whooshed by Linda's head. She looked up in time to see a small owl fly across the grasslands.

"A burrowing owl," she told Jackie. "That means 'stay on the trail.' "

"What does an owl have to do with staying on the trail?" Jackie asked.

"Burrowing owls live in holes in the ground," Marni called over her shoulder. "If a horse steps in a hole, he could break his leg."

Linda laughed. "I guess you just got lesson number two."

The owl circled beside them. Then, talons lowered like landing gear, he dropped to the earth. When he rose, a field mouse squirmed in his claws.

"Oh, gross!" Jackie said, nearly falling out of her saddle.

Linda laughed. "Hey, city slicker, welcome to the country."

Up ahead, Kathy and the others began to trot their horses.

Linda squeezed her heels against Amber's side, and the mare broke into a slow jog. Linda knew the trail was safe even in the dark. She and Kathy had ridden it many times, and by now they knew every tree and rock.

Beside her, Jackie bounced and jiggled on Copper. But Linda noted her balance looked pretty good.

"You're doing great!" she called to Jackie.

The worn path twisted and turned as the terrain grew rockier. On the right side, huge boulders gleamed in the moonlight. On the left, scrubby rabbitbrush poked through the hard earth.

Suddenly, Patches halted, and the line of horses behind him piled into one another.

"What's the problem?" Linda called out.

"Oh, great, another wild animal," Jackie groaned, clutching the pommel even tighter.

"Shhh!" Kathy hushed them. "I heard something on top of those rocks!"

"Quit trying to scare us," Linda called.

Leading Copper, she rode to the front of the line. Patches was standing stiff as a statue, staring wide-eyed at the mountain of rocks. Linda halted Amber next to the pinto. The mare snorted and nervously flicked her ears.

Kathy gulped. "There *is* something up there."

"I know," Linda whispered. "Amber hears it, too."

"Come on, guys, cut it out," Jackie begged. She

looked anxiously into the dark night. "Didn't you have enough fun with the coyotes and the owl? You're scaring me."

Suddenly, an eerie growl pierced the air. Goosebumps raced up Linda's arm, and Amber pranced in place.

"Whoa, girl," she soothed.

"What do you think it is?" Kathy whispered to Linda.

"I don't know." Linda shook her head.

"Let's get out of here!" Jackie cried. She jumped in her saddle, and one heel kicked Copper sharply. Startled, the mare lunged past Amber, pulling the lead line from Linda's grasp. Copper trotted up the path—right toward the rocks.

"Linda!" Jackie cried for help. Linda spun Amber sideways and in two leaps reached Copper. Bending over, she snatched up the lead line—just in time. The growl rang out above them.

"I know what it is," Kathy cried. "It's a mountain lion!"

"It can't be a mountain lion." Linda said quickly. "They never come this close to the ranch."

"I don't care what it is!" Jackie exclaimed. She clung to Copper's mane, her face pale with fear. "I just want to go back."

20

Linda shushed her as another growl rumbled across the rocks. Then she heard muffled laughter.

"Bob and Larry!" she muttered under her breath.

"Bob and Larry?" Kathy repeated in surprise.

"I'd bet my new boots." Linda frowned. This explained why Bob had acted so nice all afternoon, asking what the girls were going to do. Then, when Larry rode over, she should have known they'd think up a stunt like this.

"Who are Bob and Larry?" Jackie asked.

"Bob is Linda's older brother," Kathy explained.

"And Larry Spencer is his best friend—and the biggest joker in Lockwood," Marni added. "He's always playing tricks."

Linda handed Copper's lead line to Kathy. "I'm going to ride around the rocks and check this out."

All the girls stared at her in disbelief.

"But what if it *is* a mountain lion?" Jackie asked worriedly.

"Then I'll gallop back *real* fast." Linda chuckled. "You guys stay here and keep pretending to be scared." Then, clucking to Amber, she urged her horse up the path.

As Linda rode closer to the boulders, her heart

beat like a drum and the reins slipped through her sweaty fingers. She didn't feel quite as brave as she'd sounded. What if it really was a mountain lion?

Amber must have been wondering the same thing. The mare was tense with excitement. Linda patted her reassuringly.

Silently, they made their way to the far side of the rocks. Linda held her breath as they came around the huge pile. The growling had come from the top of the boulders. If Bob and Larry were making the noise, she should be able to see them from here.

Suddenly, she spotted two horses tethered to a low bush. It was Rocket, Bob's horse, and Larry's Appaloosa, Snowbird.

Linda clapped a hand to her mouth to suppress a giggle of relief. Rocket gave a low nicker when he saw his stablemate.

Quietly, Linda rode up to the horses. As she untied them, she heard a shout. Bob was looking down at her from the top of a boulder.

"Hey! What're you doing?" he cried.

Without replying, Linda grabbed both horses' reins. Then, laughing out loud, she made off with the two horses, back to the other girls.

"Look what I found!" she called triumphantly.

"So it *was* those jerks!" Kathy yelled. "And all this time we were worrying about what we should do if a mountain lion came at us."

A loud shout came from the rocks. Bob and Larry were scrambling down the side of the boulders as fast they could.

"Where are you going with those horses?" Larry yelled.

Linda laughed. "We're saving them from a pair of mountain lions," she shouted back.

Then she tossed Snowbird's reins to Marni. "Kathy, do you still have Jackie's lead line? Good. Let's get out of here before our two mountain lions get really ferocious!"

With a lot of laughter, the girls reined their horses around just as Bob and Larry jumped to the ground.

"Don't you guys dare leave us here," Bob shouted.

"If you big, strong boys don't mind mountain lions, you shouldn't care about walking a few miles to get home." Linda kicked Amber into a canter. The mare flew down the path, Rocket next to her, their hooves pounding the rocky ground. The other girls were right behind.

"Don't go so fast!" Linda heard someone cry out.

Linda looked over her shoulder. In the moonlight, she could just make out Jackie on Copper. The new girl was slumped over Copper's neck, her fingers grasping the mane tightly.

Poor Jackie! In all the excitement, Linda had forgotten all about her riding lessons.

Quickly, Linda tugged on Amber's reins. Kathy and Patches slowed behind them. Copper came to a halt, and Jackie gave a gasp of relief. "I was slipping off," she explained to the two girls with an embarrassed smile.

Kathy frowned. "The boys will catch up with us," she said, glancing back down the trail.

"I doubt it," Linda said.

Amy and Marni caught up with them, and the five riders continued down the path at a walk. When they arrived back at Rancho del Sol, Mac, the ranch foreman, was leaning against the barn door. "You ladies find some runaway horses?" he asked, a grin creasing his tanned face.

"Yeah! They were running away from a mountain lion!" Linda told him.

Laughing and joking, the girls dismounted. Linda turned to check on Jackie. She was still sitting on Copper, a doubtful look on her face. Linda wondered what the problem was now. Then it hit her. Jackie had no idea how to get off her horse!

Linda handed Rocket to Mac and, leading Amber, walked over to Copper. "Need some help?" she asked.

Jackie blushed. "Uh, right. I think now is the time for lesson number three, How to Dismount." She managed to make it sound like a joke, but Linda could hear a catch in her voice. This hadn't been an easy ride for her.

"Okay," Linda said quietly, "we'll make this as simple as possible. Put your hands on the pommel, then swing your right leg over Copper's back."

With awkward movements, Jackie followed the instructions.

"Keep your left foot in the stirrup until your right leg's on this side. It'll feel like you're standing in the stirrup."

Jackie gave her a confused glance.

"Don't worry, Copper won't run off," Linda reassured her. "Now kick your left foot free of the stirrup and jump lightly to the ground."

Losing her balance, Jackie fell backward. Linda caught her under the arm so she wouldn't fall.

"Thanks," Jackie gasped. "You guys make it look so easy."

"It'll be easy for you, too, when you've done it enough times. Just give it a chance."

Taking Copper's reins, Linda led the two horses into their stalls. As soon as Amber was settled, Linda helped Jackie. The new girl stood looking at Copper. The expression on her face was almost sad.

"Are you all right?" Linda asked.

Jackie shrugged, then started vigorously brushing Copper.

"I just checked outside and there's no sign of Larry and Bob," Marni called down the aisle.

"We'd better hurry," Linda told her friends. "They'll be here any second."

"And knowing Bob and Larry, they'll have come up with something to pay us back," Kathy added.

Quickly, the girls finished cleaning the horses. Then they peeked around the barn door.

"All clear," Linda whispered.

The five girls raced down the drive. Giggling and pushing, they dashed into the ranch kitchen, almost knocking Luisa over.

"What in the world?" the housekeeper cried.

"No time to explain," Linda said breathlessly. "Can you bring some lemonade and cookies up to my bedroom? Please?"

She ran down the hall after her friends, then turned with a grin. "And knock three times, Luisa —so we know it's you!"

3 ◆◆◆◆

For the rest of the night, the girls spent their time in Linda's room. They spread their sleeping bags on the floor, then sat on them, fooling around, giggling, and staying on guard against Bob and Larry.

"Keep your eyes open," Kathy warned, "especially when you step out of this room. I wouldn't put it past them to pull a stupid trick like sticking a frog in the toilet."

"Ick." Jackie wrinkled her nose. "I've seen enough creepy animals to last me a year."

Marni and Amy ran through their whole mirror routine, with the other girls calling out suggestions. Even Jackie got into it after a while.

Then Kathy did some gymnastics stunts that she'd been practicing. She ended with a flip that landed her neatly on her feet. "I just added that last part," she said. "Some people around here could use lessons on how to fall."

"Ha, ha, very funny," Linda said, looking at her friend. Kathy was acting a little sharp, even for fooling around. She'd taken a couple of shots at Linda and more at Jackie. What was her problem? Did she think Linda was getting too friendly?

"It's your turn, Jackie," Marni said. "What'll you be doing for the talent show?"

Jackie shrugged, all huddled up in her sleeping bag. "I don't know if I'll even be in it," she said.

"Oh, don't be silly." Amy bounced up and grabbed Jackie's guitar from the floor. "You have this, don't you? You could sing a song." She jumped in front of the other girls.

"Baby, be mine!" she sang, pretending to strum the guitar. Dressed in a baggy T-shirt, her red curls sticking at all angles, she looked like a crazy rock star.

"Give us a break!" Marni exclaimed, rolling her eyes. "Let Jackie play."

Amy handed the guitar to Jackie. She looked at it for a second as if she'd never seen it before. Then reluctantly, she set it on her lap and began to play.

"Wow," Amy whispered. "Isn't that 'Love Me Forever'?"

Linda nodded. "Jackie's really good."

When she finished playing, the girls applauded loudly.

"Boy, Jackie, you could really help Bob and Larry's band," Linda said.

"That's for sure," Marni agreed. "The coyotes we heard tonight sing better than the Hombres."

"I don't know," Jackie said. "After the trick we pulled on them, they might not be too crazy about the idea. Besides, I'm not *that* good."

"Come on, you were great," Kathy said. "I bet your folks must have shelled out a lot for lessons for you to play that well."

Abruptly, Jackie put the guitar down and stood up. "Excuse me for a minute," she said. Then she hopped over Marni's sleeping bag and disappeared into the bathroom.

"Well, pardon *me*," Kathy said. "I guess the rich girl doesn't like to talk about money."

There was a moment of embarrassed silence, then Marni sent a pillow flying at Kathy. Grinning mischievously, Kathy ducked and the pillow hit Amy. More pillows filled the air. The girls were so busy with the pillow fight that they didn't even notice when Jackie came back in.

* * *

The next morning, Linda woke with a yawn. She sat up quickly, almost knocking Kathy out of her bed. The other girls were scattered across the floor in sleeping bags.

"Everyone check to make sure there's no shaving cream in your boots or snakes in your backpacks," she warned.

Marni groaned. "I thought you said your brother couldn't get in your room."

Kathy laughed. "Knowing Bob and Larry, they'd climb two stories and shinny in the window just to get their revenge."

The girls carefully checked out their stuff. Then Amy sent a pillow flying at Linda, who had pulled on a pair of jeans. "You just said that to wake us up," she accused.

Jumping out of the way, Linda slid a T-shirt over her head, then opened the bedroom door.

"Well, it looks like it worked. You guys can stay in here all morning if you want," she said, ducking to avoid another pillow. "But I'm going downstairs for some of Luisa's pancakes."

When they heard the word "pancakes," the girls cheered and began scrambling to get dressed.

"Last one down cleans the stalls!" Linda told them. Then, chuckling, she clattered down the stairs to the dining room. Her grandmother was sipping her morning coffee.

"You're nice and early," Doña greeted her granddaughter.

"The smell of Luisa's pancakes woke me up," Linda said. She reached for a pitcher of fresh-squeezed orange juice and filled five glasses. She could hear the others stomping down the wooden steps.

"M-m-m," Kathy said hungrily as everyone crowded into the dining room and sat down. Linda passed around the plate of pancakes.

"And what's on the schedule for this morning?" Doña asked. She looked around at the five heads bent over stacks of pancakes topped with fruit and jam.

"Everyone's practicing," Linda replied. "Kelly's coming to help me with my stunt, and—"

A loud screech, then an ear-splitting twang interrupted her.

"What was that?" Jackie asked.

Linda pointed in the direction of the family room. "Bob and Larry's band."

"They should change their names to the Coyotes," Kathy said, mumbling her words through a mouthful of pancake.

"How come they're practicing so early?" Linda asked her grandmother. "They're ruining our breakfast."

Doña hid a smile in her napkin. "Larry has to work at his dad's store this afternoon."

A blast of music poured into the dining room. It sounded like ten instruments, each playing a different song. Linda held her ears, and even Doña had to laugh.

When they finished breakfast, Linda motioned her friends toward the family room. "Let's spy on them and see if we can discover their trick for sounding so terrible."

Giggling quietly, the girls tiptoed down the hall and peered around the doorway.

Bob, Larry, and their friend Jason Saunders had set up amplifiers in front of the huge stone fireplace. Bob and Larry held electric guitars. Jason sat behind a set of drums. They all looked serious.

Bob began to tap his foot and hum. He held a bass guitar. Larry, the lead guitar player, started to play. He was so awful, Linda had to put a hand over her mouth to keep from laughing.

Bob glared at her over his shoulder. "If you guys are going to hang around, then be quiet."

"Yeah, after last night, you're hardly our favorite people," Larry said.

"Oh? What happened last night?" Kathy asked in an innocent voice.

That made everyone giggle louder. The boys ignored them. Larry plucked the strings of his guitar. It screeched and whined.

"Would you do something with that thing?" Bob said. "We don't have all morning."

Larry looked at the guitar in disgust. "Ever since I bought it, I can't get the sound right. I don't know what the problem is."

"Would you like some help?"

Everybody turned and stared at Jackie. Her face went bright red, but she went on in a rush, "I mean, I know a little about guitars."

"Nah, I'll figure it out," Larry said, fiddling with the knobs below the strings. Again he strummed the guitar, and it sounded even worse.

"Larry, admit it, you need help," Bob said impatiently.

"But—" Larry protested. Linda knew the last thing he wanted was to be shown up by a girl.

"I think your amplifier needs adjusting," Jackie said quickly. She walked over to the tall, rectangular amp. "You need to change the treble."

She turned a knob on top of the amp. "Then decrease the reverb."

Linda glanced at Kathy in confusion. "Decrease the reverb?" she mouthed to her friend.

"Now try it." Jackie stepped back, almost bumping into Bob, who'd been looking over her shoulder.

Larry strummed the guitar and a smooth sound came out.

The girls clapped. "Yay, Jackie!"

"Hey, thanks," Bob said, then turned his back on her and began talking to the other guys.

"Yeah, thanks," Larry mumbled, but his mind was already on his guitar.

Jackie turned and joined her friends in the hallway.

"Typical," Linda said as they all walked through the kitchen and out the back door. "Lend them a hand, and see how they show their appreciation."

"That's all right. I did it for everyone else," Jackie said with a grin, "to save us all from going deaf."

The girls laughed.

"Hey, how'd you know all that treble and reverb stuff?" Linda asked as they strolled to the barn.

"Oh, it's no big deal," Jackie said. Then she

twirled in her tracks to face the others. "So what're we going to do now?" she added in the same breath.

"Kelly's coming so I can work on my stunt with her," Linda said. "You guys can practice your acts if you want."

"I'm watching you," Kathy said. "I can practice my gymnastics after Kelly leaves. I wouldn't miss you falling off again for anything."

"I want to watch, too," Jackie said. "Maybe it'll help me learn more about riding."

"The only thing it'll teach you is how to fall off!" Kathy added with a laugh.

They all went down the drive and into the barn. Linda quickly brushed and saddled Amber. Kelly had to work later that morning, and Linda didn't want to keep her friend waiting.

She led Amber out of the barn just as Kelly rode up the drive. As usual, the fourteen-year-old was riding her coal black mustang, Cinder, bareback. Kelly was a really good trick rider.

"Can't stay long," Kelly said breathlessly. "Mr. Manlon needs help with some calves."

"No problem," Linda said as she mounted. "But, boy, do I need help with this trick."

"It just takes time," Kelly reassured her as they

rode into the riding ring in front of the house. "First, start jumping behind me while the horses are walking."

Linda halted Amber next to Cinder, and the two horses sniffed noses. Amber pawed the ground.

"Whoa!" Linda told the mare sternly. She didn't need another pair of dusty pants!

"Now swing your right leg across Cinder's back and jump!"

This time, the trick went smoothly—Linda slid behind Kelly with no hitch.

"Okay. Now we do it at a jog. The secret is to keep the horses neck and neck at all times."

Linda jumped off Cinder. By now, an audience had lined up along the fence.

"If I fall, you guys better not laugh," she warned her friends.

Linda walked around to Amber and put her toe in the stirrup. Suddenly, the saddle slid down the palomino's side to her stomach. Linda jumped free just in time.

"Easy, girl," Linda soothed.

Kelly leapt off Cinder and helped Linda undo the girth. The saddle fell to the ground in a heap.

"Does that happen a lot?" Jackie asked, her voice worried.

"No," Linda assured her.

Another voice said with a laugh, "Next time, little sister, you'd better check your girth before you get on!"

Linda looked up. Her brother was sitting on the opposite side of the fence, grinning.

"It was you!" she accused, waving her fist in pretended anger.

He shrugged. "Maybe. Or maybe Amber lost weight last night running around with those *mountain lions*. You'll never know."

Linda laughed. Her brother certainly hadn't taken long to get even! She picked up the dusty saddle and blanket and threw them on the palomino.

"Boys," she growled.

"At least you *have* a brother," Jackie said wistfully.

The other girls stared at her as if she were crazy.

"You *want* a brother?" Kathy exclaimed.

"Hey, you can rent mine anytime," Linda said. "Cheap."

Just then, Jackie checked her watch. "Uh-oh. I have to leave. My dad's flying in this morning. Thanks for the good time, though. Really."

"Sure. Maybe we can do it again," Linda said.

Silently, the girls watched as Jackie snatched up her guitar and began to walk down the drive.

"Are you walking home?" Marni called after her.

"No, my ride's picking me up at the end of the drive."

"Hey! Look at that!" Kathy exclaimed. All of them turned. A long, white limousine was pulling up the drive. It halted beside Jackie.

A man jumped out of the driver's seat and opened the back door for Jackie.

"Oh, it's here already." Jackie gave them an embarrassed grin. "'Bye."

She raised her hand as if to wave but just as quickly dropped it. Then she ducked her head and disappeared into the backseat of the huge limousine.

4 ◆◆◆◆

The limo headed down the drive and drove from view. For a moment, no one moved.

Then Kathy broke the silence. "I thought Jackie was rich," she said, "but her father must be a millionaire. Who else would have a limo just for his kid?"

"Maybe they're going to the airport to pick up her father," Linda said. "Besides, what difference does it make if she's rich or not?"

"I'd say it makes a big difference. Look at the way Jackie didn't want to do anything with us."

"She just moved to a new place in the middle of the school year," Linda said. "She's feeling left out. I remember when I first came to Lockwood, it was hard making friends. It seemed like everyone had known one another since they were little kids."

"Well, I still say she's a snob," Kathy said stubbornly. "When she first came to school, I tried to be real friendly. All she gave me was the cold shoulder."

"Hey, look," Marni pointed at the ground by her foot. "Jackie forgot her backpack."

"Guess I'll have to take it over later," Linda said.

"Linda, I've been looking at *my* watch," Kelly said, "and I have to get to work in half an hour. Let's try the trick at a slow jog, then you can keep practicing it later with Kathy."

"Sounds good to me." Linda tightened her girth, then double-checked it. She didn't need any more accidents. Sticking her toe in the stirrup, she swung up onto Amber.

Kathy climbed onto the top board of the fence and pulled a camera from her shirt pocket. "This time if you fall, we'll have the big event on record."

Linda made a face, then clucked to Amber. Side by side, the palomino and the mustang jogged up the center of the ring.

Linda glanced over at Kelly.

"I'll signal when you should jump," the older girl said. "The horses need to be moving at the same speed and be so close their sides are touching. If one of them should slow or turn, you'll fall."

41

Linda nodded. She understood all about falling. Suddenly, Kelly motioned for her to jump. Linda kicked her feet free, ready to make her move, then suddenly froze in the saddle. What if she fell again?

With a deep breath, Linda steadied Amber. Then she dropped the reins, grabbed Kelly's shoulders with both hands, and jumped.

"Yay!" the other girls cheered as Linda landed on the mustang's broad rump.

Linda sighed with relief. Kelly cantered Cinder in a circle, halting in front of the fence. Linda slid off and whistled for Amber. When the mare jogged over, Linda gave her a big hug.

"We did it!"

"Great job! And I've got it all on film." Kathy held up the camera.

"Great. Now *everybody* can see how scared I was," Linda joked as she led Amber up to the fence.

"It's time for me to be going," Kelly said. "You did it perfectly, so just keep practicing with Kathy until we can get together again. Then we'll try it at the canter."

"I hope Patches will do as well as Cinder," Kathy said. "Otherwise, our practice sessions are going to leave Linda black and blue."

With a laugh, Kelly trotted Cinder from the ring and down the drive. The girls waved good-bye.

Marni turned to Linda. "You mean you really were scared? I thought you were fearless on horseback."

Linda shook her head. "Not when something's new." She stroked Amber's soft nose. "Now I know how Jackie feels."

The three girls looked puzzled.

Linda tried to explain. "We're so used to being around horses—we forget how big and scary they seem to city kids."

"It's like when I learned backflips," Kathy said. "At first I was terrified, but now they're easy for me."

"I guess we did kind of make her feel bad," Marni said.

"But not on purpose," Amy piped up. "I just couldn't believe she'd never been on a horse before."

"I guess we could've tried harder to help her," Marni said.

"Hey, enough about Jackie," Kathy interrupted. "I need some ideas for my gymnastics act. What kind of music should I use for my routine?" She jumped off the fence.

"You could've used Jackie's help with that."
Marni grinned. "She's the musical one."

"Yeah, that's all I need," Kathy said.

"I guess you're right." Linda led Amber out the
gate. "Of course," she added with a twinkle, "you
could get Bob and Larry to help."

"Some choice," Kathy complained. "When the
Hombres played this morning, it sounded like chalk
squeaking on a blackboard!"

"Looks like your friends had a great time," Doña
Mallory said that evening. She and Linda were
seated around the dining table finishing an early
dinner.

Bronco, Linda's grandfather, was away for the
weekend on business. Bob had gone into
Lockwood to practice with his band.

"We did have a good time," Linda told her
grandmother. "Thanks for letting me have the girls
over. We got in a lot of practice. You should see
everyone's acts. They're really neat."

"I saw part of yours. It looked dangerous. When
I gave you permission, I didn't know these stunts
would be so tricky."

"Don't worry. Kelly's a really good teacher."

44

Linda gulped the rest of her milk. "May I be excused?"

"No dessert?" Doña pretended to be shocked.

"I'll have some later. I need to ride over to Jackie Lee's house and drop off her backpack. I tried to call, but the operator said it was an unlisted number."

"Jackie's the new friend you invited?"

Linda nodded. "Yes. She seems pretty nice—I guess."

Doña gave her a questioning look.

"It's hard to explain," Linda said. "The others don't seem to like her much. And Kathy acts almost jealous. But I—I guess I feel sort of sorry for her. She just moved here from Los Angeles, and she seems pretty lonely."

"Then it's nice you invited her," Doña said. "Where does she live?"

"Lucky Star Ranch."

"I'm glad someone finally bought that place. It's been vacant for almost two years. The house is so big and expensive that most folks weren't interested."

"Maybe I'll get to go inside." Linda gave her grandmother a quick kiss good-bye.

"Just be home before dark," Doña cautioned.

Picking up her glass and plate, Linda headed into the kitchen, then out to the barn.

She'd already fed and brushed Amber, so the mare was ready for a ride. Linda carried the saddle and bridle over to the stall. As soon as Amber saw her, she shoved the unlatched door with her nose and stepped into the aisle. Linda tugged on her mane.

"Hey! Wait till I put the bridle on." She slipped the curb bit into Amber's mouth and slid the headstall over her ears. Then she smoothed the silky white forelock over the star on the mare's forehead.

She'd been tacking up horses for so long, she could do it with her eyes shut. Maybe if Jackie had a chance to practice a few more times, she'd find out how easy it was, too.

Linda walked Amber from the barn. The sun was low in the sky, but it was still bright out. There was plenty of time to make Lucky Star Ranch.

She tied Jackie's backpack to her saddle, then mounted. As soon as Amber realized they weren't headed for the riding ring, her ears pricked forward and she stepped out eagerly.

Linda had to laugh. Maybe she was overdoing

practice, but they were a long way from performing in front of an audience, and the talent show was only three weeks away.

Squeezing her calves against Amber's side, Linda signaled the mare to jog. They headed into a grove of walnut trees, then followed a wide stream. This was one of Linda's favorite trails. Amber splashed into the stream, her hooves spraying water into the air. She leapt up the bank, and Linda reined her to the right. Lucky Star Ranch was another mile to the east.

When they reached open pasture, Linda sat forward and clucked. Immediately, Amber stretched her legs into a smooth lope.

They cantered along a jeep trail, the warm air whistling past them. Up ahead, Linda could see Lucky Star Ranch.

Like most Southern California ranches, the main house was surrounded by whitewashed outbuildings and groves of trees. But unlike most ranches, there was a high adobe wall circling the buildings like a fortress.

This was the first time Linda had been so close to the ranch. It was hidden from the main road, and she'd only caught glimpses of it from Rancho del Sol's boundary. As she rode closer, she could see

47

that Doña was right—it was huge! The house seemed to stretch on and on forever. She wondered how Jackie ever found her way around.

Linda cantered Amber down the drive. With a gentle tug, she halted the mare in front of the arched, wrought-iron gate. It was bolted shut. She looked around, hoping to find a bell or buzzer.

Suddenly two men appeared behind the wrought-iron bars. Linda jumped in surprise. Both men were dressed in business suits, as if they'd just stepped from a downtown office.

"Hello," Linda stammered, not sure what was going on. "Uh . . . this is Lucky Star Ranch, isn't it?"

Both men gave her the once-over. Finally, the taller one unlocked the gate and stuck his head out.

"State your business."

"I'm a friend of Jackie Lee's," she said. "I have something for her." She reached behind her and untied the backpack. "Jackie left this last night. She was at my house for a party." She held it out.

The tall man plucked the pack from her hand and began searching through it.

Finally, he looked up. "We'll make sure she gets it."

"Can I give it to her myself?" Linda asked.

A Horse for Jackie

"No," the man said curtly. "We'll make sure she gets it. Now, why don't you and your horse head on home, little girl. It's getting dark."

"But I want to ask Jackie about riding with me again. And I don't know her phone number so—"

"No 'buts' about it," the man interrupted. He grabbed Amber's bridle and turned her around. The mare pinned back her ears.

"But Jackie's my—"

"It's time to go!" The second man stepped forward. "This is private property. And the owners don't like uninvited guests."

He lifted his arm high and, clucking loudly, slapped Amber on the rump.

"Hey!" Linda protested. Startled by the slap, Amber shot forward, almost throwing Linda from the saddle.

"Whoa," she hollered, grabbing the pommel just in time.

Immediately, Amber halted. She swished her tail and champed nervously on the bit. Linda laid a soothing hand on the mare's neck.

"That's okay, girl. It's not your fault."

She swung around in the saddle to tell the two guys off. But they'd disappeared and the gate was shut tight.

"Weird," she muttered.

A rustle in the bushes by the gate caught her attention. Curious, she urged Amber closer. The mare pricked her ears and took a cautious step toward the thorny plants.

Linda could just make out the outline of a man. He was kneeling behind the bushes, his back pressed against the adobe wall.

Suddenly, he pointed something at her. Linda heard a click, then the flash of a bright light blinded her.

Startled by the light, Amber twirled on her hind legs and leapt sideways. Linda blinked, but all she could see were spots.

"Whoa, Amber. Whoa!" She pulled roughly on the reins. Amber slid to a stop.

Linda blinked again. Amber had halted inches away from a barbed-wire fence.

Thank goodness the mare had stopped in time. The fence surrounded an old orchard. It was overgrown with weeds and prickly bushes, but the rusty wire strands were a lot more dangerous, especially since they were hard to see.

Linda stroked Amber's sweaty neck, then turned toward Rancho del Sol. She wasn't even curious about the man in the bushes. She realized that the

A Horse for Jackie

glaring light had to have come from a flash camera, but she didn't want to find out why he wanted her picture. Linda just wanted to be as far away from Lucky Star Ranch as she could.

She clucked and Amber broke into a canter.

"*Un*lucky Star Ranch," Linda muttered as the mare eagerly made for home. "That's what it should be called."

5 ♦♦♦♦

"Hey, Jackie!" Linda ran down the main hall of the school the next afternoon, trying to catch up to her friend. Jackie had darted out of the classroom so fast, Linda hadn't gotten a chance to talk to her about the previous night.

Turning, Jackie waited.

"Did you get your backpack?" she asked.

"Yeah. Thanks."

Linda walked beside her as they pushed their way down the crowded hall. "What's the story with those two goons at the gate?"

Jackie shrugged. "My dad likes his privacy. You know how it is."

No, I don't, Linda wanted to say. She didn't know anyone who had guards at their gate.

"When I left," Linda continued, "there was

some guy hiding in the bushes. I think he took my picture."

Jackie stopped and stared at her. "He did what?" She almost looked scared.

"I thought *you* could tell me about that," Linda said.

"Well, I can't." Jackie abruptly turned and pushed open the school doors. Linda hurried after her.

"Wait. There's something else I have to ask. Do you want to go riding again? I thought maybe I could give you another lesson this afternoon."

Linda had figured Jackie would jump at the chance. So when Jackie hesitated, Linda was a little confused.

"I thought *you* *wanted* to ride," she said.

"Oh, I do!" Jackie quickly spoke up. "It's not that. It's . . ."

Linda waited, curious to hear what was the problem. But Jackie only gnawed her lip.

"Okay," Jackie finally said.

"Great." Linda smiled as they boarded the schoolbus.

They pushed their way down the aisle, then sat together in the last seat.

Jackie's stop was first. "I'll be over as soon as

I change clothes," she called, heading for the door.

When the bus pulled away, Jackie waved to Linda excitedly, a huge smile on her face.

The bus halted at the end of the Mallorys' drive. Bronco was waiting for Linda in the jeep. Linda hadn't seen him since Friday morning.

"Thought you might like a lift," he said.

Linda hugged her handsome, silver-haired grandfather over the door of the jeep.

"We missed you!" she exclaimed. Dashing around to the other side, she climbed in beside him. Bronco smiled and ruffled her hair.

"And I missed you!" he said. "Not to mention all the excitement I missed."

"Excitement?" Linda asked innocently as the jeep started up.

Bronco's laugh was big and booming. "Doña told me a mountain lion was spotted just a mile from here." He winked at Linda, and it was her turn to laugh.

After she'd told him the whole story, Linda mentioned Jackie. "Have you met Mr. Lee? The new owner of Lucky Star Ranch?" she asked. "Or at least, have you heard anything about him?"

He thought a minute. "Can't say I have."

"That's strange. You usually know everybody in Lockwood."

"Not *everybody*," he protested with a chuckle. "This Mr. Lee may work somewhere else. Lots of folks seem to be doing that these days." He halted the jeep in front of the ranch house, then turned to Linda. "But why all the questions?"

She shrugged. "Jackie seems very secretive about her dad, and I don't know why."

"Well, give her time." He ruffled her hair again.

Just then, Doña bustled from the house. Bronco's face lit up, and he jumped from the jeep to greet his wife.

Linda waved hello to her grandmother, then ran into the ranch house and up to her bedroom. Quickly, she changed into her work jeans and cowboy boots.

"Linda!" her grandmother called up the steps. "Jackie's here."

Linda clattered down the steps, tucking in her shirt as she ran.

She found Jackie in the family room, standing next to Bob, strumming on his guitar. Jackie listened and fiddled with the knobs on the amplifier, trying to get the right sound.

"Hi!" Linda called. "Ready to ride?"

"Give her a minute," Bob said before Jackie could answer.

Jackie hummed a tune and strummed the deep-sounding bass.

"That sounds a lot better," Bob told her. "Thanks."

"No problem." Jackie smiled as she handed the guitar back to Linda's brother. "Who plays the synthesizer?" she asked, pointing to an instrument that looked like a piano keyboard.

"A friend of mine sold it to me—after he quit the band," Bob replied, his head bent over his guitar. Suddenly, he looked up. "Hey, you don't by any chance . . ." His voice trailed off.

"Play the synthesizer?" Jackie said with a grin. Bob nodded.

"As a matter of fact, I do."

"No kidding? Would you like to play with us in the talent show? We really need someone."

Jackie's face lighted up. "Sure!"

Bob got a little flustered. "Well, maybe I should ask the other guys first."

Linda could hardly believe her ears. Bob was actually asking this girl he hardly knew to join his precious band. He must be getting really desperate.

"I understand," Jackie said quickly. "And it's all right if they say no."

"You wouldn't be able to *sing* by any chance?" Bob said in a hopeful voice.

"You ought to hear her!" Linda replied.

"Great! Maybe you can play with us tomorrow, you know, just to see how the guys like you."

"Sounds good to me," Jackie said enthusiastically. She turned and walked out the door with Linda.

"Your career is launched," Linda teased as they headed toward the barn.

Jackie giggled. "Oh, it might be fun."

Amber whinnied when she heard Linda enter. She was in her stall, escaping the hot afternoon sun. Linda knew the mare would be disappointed when she didn't saddle her up. That is, until she was turned out into a field of lush grass!

"Why don't you start brushing Copper," Linda said to Jackie. "I have to let Amber out." The palomino stuck her head over the stall door and blew softly against Linda's cheek. Then she nuzzled her shirt pocket.

Linda laughed. "Boy, I can't fool you!" she said, plucking a piece of carrot from her pocket. She'd hidden the treat in her back pocket. Still, Amber had found it in no time.

Linda slipped Amber's halter on, then snapped a lead line to the back ring of the halter. The mare followed her quietly from the barn to the pasture, but as soon as Linda opened the gate and unsnapped the lead line, Amber kicked up her heels and raced across the field.

Twisting and turning, Amber frolicked like a kid on the last day of school. She pawed at shadows and snorted at blowing leaves. Then, just as suddenly, she dropped her head and hungrily tore at the green grass.

Laughing at her horse's silly behavior, Linda walked back into the barn. Jackie was combing Copper's flaxen mane.

Linda picked up a brush and joined Jackie in the stall. For a second, Jackie watched how Linda flicked the brush to get out the dirt and loose hair. Then Jackie started on Copper's other side.

The chestnut mare quit chewing her hay. Lifting her lip in the air, she wiggled it to and fro. Jackie squealed with laughter.

"What's she doing?" she asked.

"Telling us she loves to be brushed," Linda said,

pulling a hoof pick from her back pocket. "Now let me show you how to clean out her hooves."

Wide-eyed with interest, Jackie watched as Linda ran her hand down Copper's right leg. Immediately, the mare picked up her foot.

"Hold the pick in your left hand while you scrape out the dirt," she said. She dropped the mare's foot and straightened. "Now you try it."

"Okay!" Jackie said enthusiastically. Following Linda's directions, she carefully cleaned out the hoof.

Linda went into the tack room to get the bridle.

"Let me do it this time," Jackie said eagerly, taking the bridle.

With a frown of concentration, Jackie put the bit into Copper's mouth.

"I did it!" she exclaimed. She was so excited, she let go of the bridle. The bit fell from Copper's mouth.

Linda laughed. "Don't forget to put the headstall over her ears," she reminded her. "Then buckle the throatlatch."

Giggling with embarrassment, Jackie tried again. This time she did everything right.

"Great!" Linda applauded. Jackie beamed. As

they led Copper from the barn, Jackie asked breathlessly, "Listen, Linda, do you think you can teach me to canter by the day of the talent show?"

Linda hesitated. "I don't know. That's less than three weeks away," she said doubtfully. "I mean, you just learned how to put on the bridle."

Jackie grabbed her arm. "I'll work real hard. I promise."

"It doesn't have anything to do with working hard. It takes time. There's a lot to learn."

"With your help, I know I can do it," Jackie insisted.

Linda halted Copper in the middle of the riding ring. Jackie stroked the mare's nose. She gave Linda a half-excited, half-pleading look.

"Why do you want to canter before the talent show?" Linda asked.

"Because my father'll be home that weekend. He's arranging his schedule just to be here."

"Can't you just show him how well you trot?"

Jackie shook her head, then clasped her hands together. "Please. Don't say no. I want a horse so badly. It's important that my dad sees I can ride well enough to have one of my own."

"Oh, all right," Linda said in a gasp of breath.

Jackie jumped in the air, then hugged Copper around the neck. "Thanks! And you won't regret it."

"And don't you forget those guitar lessons," Linda reminded Jackie as she showed her how to mount. "If you're going to canter in time for the talent show, then I should be able to play my favorite song!"

"It's a deal," Jackie said from on top of Copper. She gathered her reins into her right hand, then smiled proudly. "See? I remembered!"

Linda hid a smile. "You did. And now we're up to lesson number four, How to Make Your Horse Walk."

"I hope I do better than I did with How to Bridle Your Horse." Jackie laughed.

"You will. Copper's very well trained. She responds to voice commands along with a gentle squeeze of your heels."

"Okay." Jackie looked serious. "Here goes. Walk."

Obediently, Copper moved from the center of the ring.

Jackie looked over her shoulder, a grin from ear to ear. "That was easy!"

"Now remember how you neck rein," Linda called. "If you're turning to the right, touch the reins to the left side of Copper's neck."

Linda watched as Jackie steered Copper to the rail. Her friend sat straight, yet relaxed. Her heels were down, and her elbows were by her side. A good start.

"Now turn to the left. Remember to keep your right heel in Copper's side if you're turning to the left."

"That doesn't make any sense." Jackie wrinkled her nose. "But Copper seems to understand."

For about ten minutes, Jackie rode Copper around the ring. Linda made her do a figure eight, then halt.

"I think I'm ready to jog," Jackie finally said.

"I'd better lead you first," Linda suggested. "It's a lot different than walking."

"No way." Jackie shook her head. "The other night, we jogged on the trail. Besides, I think I've got the hang of riding now."

"All right. But if you feel yourself falling, grab the saddlehorn and tell Copper 'Whoa.'"

Jackie nodded and tightened her grip on the reins.

"All you have to do is squeeze your heels against Copper's side."

"That's it?"

"That's it. But don't forget about steering."

Jackie kicked the chestnut lightly. Responding instantly, Copper picked up a slow, easy jog. But like all first riders, Jackie had trouble sitting to the movement of the horse. She bounced in the air, then hit the saddle hard.

Losing her balance, she fell forward onto the pommel.

"Tell Copper to whoa," Linda instructed. Jackie only clutched the saddlehorn harder. She was doubled over Copper's neck.

"Jackie!" Linda called louder. "Tell Copper to whoa!"

Jackie opened her mouth, but nothing came out. As she bounced and jostled in the saddle, her heels began to bang against Copper's sides.

Obediently, Copper trotted faster. Her strides grew longer, and Jackie began to slip sideways.

Linda walked quickly toward Copper. If she didn't hurry and stop the horse, Jackie was going to fall!

6 ♦♦♦♦

"Copper, whoa!" Linda yelled as loud as she could.

Hearing the command, the mare flicked her ears, but she didn't slow down. Linda knew Copper was obeying only her rider, and Jackie's feet continued to bang against the horse's sides.

With an outstretched hand, Linda approached the horse. Copper jogged up the side of the ring toward her.

Talking softly, Linda stepped into the horse's path. She didn't dare frighten the mare. Jackie was slumped sideways in the saddle, and any abrupt movement would throw her off.

"Hey, Copper, whoa, girl," Linda crooned. The mare eyed her curiously, then began to slow. As she started to jog past her, Linda reached out and grasped the dangling reins.

"Whoa!" She tugged sharply, and Copper stopped dead. Linda grabbed Jackie's leg to keep her from sliding off.

"Jackie? Are you all right?" Linda asked anxiously.

Jackie nodded, then slowly straightened in the saddle. "Boy, if I'd known it was that hard, I would've let you lead me. It felt like Copper was running a race."

"You didn't do so badly."

"I was really scared."

"You just took it too fast," Linda told her. "Which is my fault. I never should have let you trot alone."

"It's not your fault. It's just hopeless. I'll never learn."

Jackie plunked her hands on Copper's neck and swung her right leg over the mare's rump to dismount. At the same instant, her left toe slipped from the stirrup. With a cry, she fell backward on top of Linda.

The two girls tumbled to the ground, Jackie landing on Linda's lap. For a second, they both lay sprawled at Copper's feet.

"See what I mean!" Jackie wailed. Copper turned to stare at them with her big brown eyes. Then Linda started to giggle. Jackie slid off her friend's lap and stood up. She gave Linda a curious look.

"What's so funny?" she asked as she brushed the dust off her jeans.

Linda shook her head. She really didn't know. Maybe it was the fact that lately she'd spent an awful lot of time on the ground.

"My poor rear's going to be black and blue," she said. Jackie frowned, not sure what she meant.

Linda picked herself up and dusted off her pants. "This is the third time I've hit the dirt in one week," she explained.

"You fell off again?" Jackie asked, incredulous.

"Oh, yeah. A good one, too. I missed Patches' rump and landed flat on my back."

"You weren't scared to get back on?"

"No. But I was scared to try the trick again. I felt so dumb. You know—not being able to do it."

Jackie took the reins from Linda's fingers. "Then I guess I can get back on, too."

Linda grinned. "Good. Only this time, I'll lead you around first. Until you get the hang of it."

"Sounds good to me." With a deep breath, Jackie mounted.

Linda put her hand loosely on Copper's bridle and led her to the rail. "You give her the signal to jog whenever you're ready."

She could hear Jackie inhale, then exhale with a rush. "Jog," she finally said, and Copper moved out.

Linda ran beside the mare, calling instructions over her shoulder. When Jackie began to bounce, she told her to pretend she was a sack of potatoes. "You want to sit kind of heavy. Don't fight the movement. Go with it."

Halfway around, she glanced over her shoulder. She could see that Jackie was less rigid. Her body bobbed up and down, but she wasn't slipping sideways. She even had a smile on her face.

Linda let go of Copper's bridle and dropped back next to Jackie's leg.

"How's it feel?" she called up to her.

"Better! I like it."

"When you're ready to stop, just tug gently on the reins and tell Copper to walk."

They jogged up to the fence, then Jackie gave Copper the command. The mare stopped immediately.

Bending over the saddlehorn, Jackie threw her arms around the chestnut's neck. "I love this horse!" she cried.

Linda laughed. "Aren't you glad you tried again?"

Jackie nodded. "Thanks," she said quietly. "I know it must seem stupid to you—getting so scared over a horse trotting."

Silently, she dismounted, this time landing on her feet.

"It just takes time," Linda said.

"I guess."

Together they led Copper back to her stall. Linda showed Jackie how to undo the girth and take off the bridle.

"Copper's a little sweaty, so we should sponge her off," Linda said, fetching a bucket. She sloshed a sponge in the water, then splashed it on the back of the chestnut horse.

"It's just that my dad still thinks I'm a little kid," Jackie explained. "Whenever I ask him about a horse, he says, 'But you can't even ride.' That's his way of saying 'Forget it.'"

She sighed. "He thinks horses are dangerous. He's always telling me I could break my neck falling off a horse. That's probably why I freaked out when Copper started going fast.

"And I want a horse *so* badly," Jackie continued. "My dad's away so much, he doesn't realize— But if I had a horse like Amber, I wouldn't get so lonely."

"Where's your mom?" Linda picked up the bucket and walked around to Copper's other side.

"New York City. My parents are divorced. I can visit her any time, but I hate cities." Jackie wrinkled her nose. "In fact, I was the one who suggested to my dad that we move from Los Angeles."

"Are you sorry you moved?" Linda asked.

"No—except I don't get to see my dad so much. That makes it pretty lonely. I guess you wouldn't understand that—you have *everything*," Jackie added in a rush.

"Not everything." Linda's voice got tight. "I suppose nobody told you—my parents are dead."

Jackie stared at Linda. "I—I didn't know," she stammered. "I mean, I knew your grandparents lived here, but—"

Linda gave her an understanding smile as she unlatched the stall door. "It's okay," she said. "I'm happy living with Bronco and Doña. But if you

ever want to talk about your dad, I'll understand."
She tossed the lead line to Jackie.

"Thanks. And I think you *would* understand. I guess I'm no different from any kid whose parents are divorced. I shuttle back and forth between them. Of course, living with my dad, I get to see him a lot more. I just wish . . ." Her voice trailed off.

Linda paused and looked up at Jackie. Her friend was staring off into space, absently stroking Copper's neck.

Just as quickly, Jackie's face brightened. "I really did enjoy the lesson. Do you think I could have another one tomorrow?"

Linda grinned. "We're not finished with this one yet." She picked up a long metal object. "This is a sweat scraper. It whisks the water off Copper's back so she'll dry faster." Linda showed how the scraper worked. "Here, you try it. Then we need to walk Copper for a few minutes to cool her off."

"Boy, I never knew horses needed so much care," Jackie said as she ran the scraper along Copper's side. "But it seems more like fun than work."

Ten minutes later, the white limousine pulled up

in front of the barn. Linda could see it from the barn aisle—it filled the doorway.

"Your ride's here," she said.

Jackie was still in Copper's stall, combing the horse's silky mane.

"So soon?" Jackie sighed. She kissed the mare on her neck and walked into the aisle. "I hate to leave—I was having so much fun."

Suddenly, she turned around. "Hey—why don't you come home with me? We can fix sandwiches, and I'll give you your first official guitar lesson."

"I don't know." Linda hesitated. Bob had offered to help her practice her stunt. Then she rubbed her aching bottom. Maybe a day off wouldn't be a bad idea. "Okay—let me ask my grandmother."

She ran from the barn, past the limousine, and up the drive.

"Any homework?" Doña asked when Linda finally found her in the ranch office.

Linda shook her head, and her grandmother gave her permission to go with Jackie.

"Just be home by eight," Doña added. "I know Bronco would like to spend some time with you. He's curious about the stunt you're practicing for the talent show."

"Okay," Linda called over her shoulder. She didn't have time to change clothes, but Jackie was just as grubby.

The limo was in front of the ranch house, its motor running. Linda couldn't see anything through the tinted windows, but then Jackie opened the door.

"Slide in," she said.

The backseat was so long, the two of them barely took up any room. Linda ran her hands over the maroon leather seats.

"Thirsty?" Jackie asked as she flipped open a compartment. She pulled out two frosty mugs and a couple of sodas.

Linda nodded. This was luxury! While Jackie poured, Linda peered toward the front seat. She knew the driver was up there, but she couldn't see a thing through the tinted glass that separated them. It was almost as if the car were running itself.

When they got to Lucky Star Ranch, the gates opened automatically. There was no sign of the two guards. The limo cruised around a circular drive and halted in front of the house.

Jackie jumped out. "I don't know about you, but I'm starved."

"Me, too. I could eat a horse!" Linda grinned at

Jackie, remembering what she'd said the other night at the party. Giggling, the two girls raced up the steps.

Jackie opened a huge carved-wood door, and Linda entered a spacious hallway. The house was built and decorated in the same Spanish style as Rancho del Sol, but it must have been three times as big.

Jackie led the way down a maze of hallways to the kitchen. It was the size of the Mallorys' family room and filled with every possible appliance.

"Luisa would really love this," Linda said.

The two girls made tuna sandwiches and talked a while about school. They were cleaning up their dishes when an older woman peeked in on them. Her gray hair was cut short, and she wore a friendly smile.

Jackie introduced Linda, then said, "This is Greta, my—" She paused, a grin on her face. "Just what are you, Greta?" she asked playfully.

"How about the person who tucks you in at night?" Greta suggested.

"Thanks." Jackie laughed. "Now Linda will think I sleep with a teddy bear, too."

"Oh, I wouldn't give away all your secrets," Greta said. She pointed to a cookie jar. "You girls

73

wouldn't by any chance like some lemonade and cookies?"

They both nodded eagerly. Jackie reached into the jar and grabbed a handful for both of them.

"Have a good time, girls," Greta said as she left. "And call me if you need anything." The kitchen door swung closed behind her.

Jackie picked up her plate. "Greta's great, but she's also part of my problem," she said in a low voice. "She's my unofficial grandmother. And she thinks horses should be only in cowboy movies."

Jackie motioned for Linda to follow her. "Come on, we can eat in the game room."

They twisted and turned down several hallways, finally ending up in a high-ceilinged room. There was a pool table in the middle of the floor, and two video games blinked and flashed in the corner.

Jackie plopped down on the sofa. Her guitar was leaning against the cushions. She took a bite of cookie, then picked up the guitar and strummed it.

Linda settled on the rug, her plate balanced in her lap.

"Tell me what you think of this song," Jackie said. She began to play and sing, her voice rich and clear over the strumming.

Linda didn't recognize the song, but when Jackie

finished, she clapped enthusiastically. "That was terrific—did you write it?"

Jackie nodded, then handed over the guitar. "It's your turn," she said.

Linda held the guitar awkwardly, not sure what to do.

Jackie laughed. "Now you know how I feel when I try to bridle Copper." Jumping from the sofa, she knelt next to Linda. "Let me show you where to put your fingers."

"This doesn't look like it's going to be easy," Linda said. "I think I'll refuel on lemonade."

"Sure—it's in the fridge." Jackie took the guitar and began to strum softly.

Linda got up and headed down the hallway. Halfway down, she realized she didn't know where she was going.

"Which door?" she called back to Jackie.

"The one on the left."

Linda turned and pushed open a swinging door.

"Wait!" Jackie hollered, scrambling to her feet. "That's the wrong way!"

7 ◆◆◆◆

Instantly, Linda realized her mistake. The room was filled with musical instruments, sound equipment, and microphones.

"Neat stuff," Linda said as Jackie rushed in behind her. "Somebody must really be into music." Curious, she stepped toward a neon-red electric guitar. Jackie caught her elbow and began steering her toward the door.

"I thought you wanted some lemonade?" she said in a tense voice.

Linda looked at her friend. Jackie's mouth was set in a straight line. Obviously, she didn't want Linda in this room.

"Sorry," Linda apologized, quickly backing out the door.

"That's the kitchen." Jackie pointed across the hall.

"Oh, yeah. I turned to *my* left instead of yours." Linda laughed at her mistake.

Jackie laughed with her, but it sounded a little strained. Linda wondered what was going on.

Pushing open the kitchen doors, Jackie darted to the refrigerator and pulled out the whole pitcher of lemonade. "Now, how about that guitar lesson?" she said with a cheery smile.

Linda was getting used to Jackie's changing moods, but it was hard having a friend with secrets. When Jackie had invited her to Lucky Star Ranch, Linda had hoped to get to know her better. Instead, she'd ended up with more questions.

The two girls made their way back to the family room. Linda quickly finished her cookies while Jackie showed her a few chords on the guitar.

"I really should go," Linda said, standing up.

"So soon?"

Linda nodded. "I have to get back and feed Amber." That *was* true, she told herself. But she was ready to leave, as well. Somehow, the evening wasn't much fun anymore.

Jackie sighed. "I wish you could stay," she said. "But I understand."

"I'll call Bronco."

"That's okay. The limo can run you home."

They made their way through the spacious house. Linda noticed that most of the rooms were dark, and it was so quiet she could hear her footsteps echoing down the hall.

Jackie opened the front door for Linda. From out of nowhere, the limo pulled to the foot of the steps and stopped.

"I had a great time," Linda said.

"Me, too."

Linda jumped down the steps and climbed into the limo. As it pulled away, she looked back through the tinted window. Jackie stood in the doorway, a sad expression on her face. Linda was sorry to leave her in the big, lonely house.

When the limo dropped her off at Rancho del Sol, Linda dashed into the barn. It was dark outside, and the barn lights glowed softly.

She grabbed a lead line and went to the back pasture. Amber was waiting patiently by the gate. She nickered and tossed her head when she saw Linda.

"Had enough grass?" Linda asked as she

snapped the lead line onto the halter. She unlatched the gate, and Amber pushed it open with her nose.

Linda reached up and hugged the palomino. She buried her face in the mare's silky mane and sighed. Horses were certainly less complicated than new friends, she thought.

With a pat, she led Amber into the barn. In one of the stalls, her brother was brushing Rocket.

Linda stopped and peered around the stall door. "So, how's band practice going? Did Larry ever get his guitar to stop screeching?"

"Yep. So now you can just call us the hottest group around."

Linda tried to keep from giggling. With his wrinkled jeans and cowboy hat pushed back on his blond hair, Bob hardly looked the part of a rock star.

"In fact," Bob added, "record producers from all over Los Angeles have been calling us night and day."

"Oh? Are they begging you not to play?" Linda asked with a straight face.

Bob gave her a look. "You just wait. I predict we'll be the winning act at the talent show."

"Not unless Larry gets laryngitis."

"He won't have to. I've convinced the guys to let Jackie audition for the band. If she's as good as you say, she can be our lead singer."

"They're letting Jackie audition?" Linda was surprised.

"Sure. She really seems to know her stuff. We could use someone like her."

"I'll say. She's good enough to have her own music room jammed full of expensive-looking equipment."

Bob stopped brushing Rocket. "No kidding? I wonder if she'd let us practice over there one day."

Linda shook her head. "I doubt it. She didn't even want me *looking* at the stuff."

Bob grinned. "That's not so strange. She was probably afraid you'd put your foot through the middle of a drum."

Linda ignored his kidding. "It was more than that," she murmured, mostly to herself.

"The band's getting together after school tomorrow," Bob went on. "She can audition then."

"Okay, Jackie," Bob said. "We're going to play the song 'Movin' On' in the key of A. You come in when you're ready. Larry? Jason? Let's hit it."

As the trio began to play, Linda leaned back

against the sofa, listening. Since Larry had adjusted his guitar he didn't sound quite as awful. Bob was pretty good on the bass, and Jason put lots of energy into the drums. But still, they needed something to make them sound like a real band. She wondered if Jackie could help pull them together.

For a moment or two, her friend just listened, her face intent as she concentrated on the music. Then she began to play the synthesizer's keyboard.

Linda couldn't believe her ears. First it sounded like Jackie was playing the drums, then she switched to a piano sound, then a guitar. And each time she changed, it added something to the harmony.

Bob grinned, and even Larry nodded his head. Then Jackie adjusted her mike and began to sing.

" 'I'm movin' on, headed home, tired of this need to roam . . .' "

As Jackie sang, Linda couldn't help but tap her feet and sway. Jackie was great.

When the band played its last chord, Linda clapped and whistled. Bob reached over the synthesizer, grabbed Jackie's hand, and shook it. "You're hired."

Jackie beamed. Linda was glad everything had

worked out. She'd never seen her new friend so happy.

"Jackie freaked out just because you went into a room full of *music* equipment?" Kathy asked Linda a week later. It was the first time Linda had told the story to anyone other than Bob.

The two girls were walking down the school hallway to the gym. They'd stayed after school so Kathy could show Linda her gymnastics routine for the talent show.

"She didn't exactly freak out," Linda explained. "She just seemed—well, different."

"That doesn't surprise me. I've been telling you all along she's weird," Kathy said. "One minute she acts like your friend, the next minute she hardly knows you."

Linda shook her head. "She's usually not that way around me."

"Oh? That's not the way it sounded."

"I just think something's bugging her. Maybe it has to do with her mysterious father."

Kathy stepped inside the school's huge gym. "Mysterious father? Are you keeping a secret from me?" She slid off her shirt and jeans. Underneath, she was wearing a bright blue leotard.

"No. I'm just putting two and two together. I figure Jackie's dad must be a hotshot record producer or something. That might explain the guards at the gate that day."

"Or it may explain why Jackie's so strange," Kathy said. "It runs in her family." She began pulling mats toward the center of the gym.

"She's not strange," Linda protested. "You ought to hear her playing with the band. Around the guys she's like a different person. And all week long I've been giving her riding lessons, and we've had fun."

"Well, I'm *so* glad you've been having so much fun with Jackie Lee," Kathy said, her hands on her hips. "But do you think you could stop talking about her long enough to watch my routine?"

She said it so sarcastically, it suddenly dawned on Linda that Kathy was really jealous. And no wonder. Linda had been spending so much time with Jackie, she hadn't even had a chance to watch her best friend's act.

She ran over and helped Kathy lift a mat. "Of course—I'm dying to see it. Marni said your flips are super."

Kathy stared as if she were wondering what Linda was up to.

"Look, Kathy, no one will ever replace you as my *best* friend," Linda assured her. "You know that, don't you?"

Her friend suddenly smiled. "I know," she admitted. Then, arching her back, she did a perfect backflip.

"I don't know how you do that. It looks painful." Linda slid a music tape into a cassette recorder.

"It's not any worse than falling off a horse," Kathy kidded.

"I haven't fallen off all week." Linda laughed. She turned on the music and listened. "Hey, good choice."

"Jackie picked it out." Kathy did a few warm-up stretches. "She helped Amy and Marni add a really funny part to their skit, too."

"See?" Linda said. "I told you she was nice. And you ought to hear her sing with the Hombres. Fortunately, she even drowns out Larry."

Kathy laughed. She walked over to the edge of the mats, then signaled Linda that she was ready.

Linda rewound the tape and turned on the player. Then she settled back against the wall to watch.

Gracefully, her friend danced across the mats. She somersaulted into a handstand and flipped backward. Landing on her feet, she immediately cartwheeled across the mat, ending with a flip in the air.

"Bravo! Bravo!" Linda clapped as Kathy bowed. Breathless, her friend raced up.

"Well? What do you think?"

"I think you're ready for the Olympics."

Kathy laughed. "Not quite." She took a walk around the gym to cool off while Linda put back the mats.

"How about a soda to celebrate?" Linda said when she was finished. "We can stop at the drugstore."

"Do you have time?" Kathy asked as she dressed.

Linda nodded. "I'm supposed to call Bronco when I need a ride."

Laughing and talking, they left the school. As they walked into town, Linda told Kathy how her act was going.

"Kelly and I practiced a lot this week. And believe it or not, I can jump onto Cinder's back while we're cantering."

"Wow, that sounds hard."

"It is," Linda said seriously. "It took me ages to learn. And there's more."

"I thought the jump was the grand finale. What else are you doing?"

"Well . . ." Linda paused. "It'll be a surprise."

Kathy stopped in front of the drugstore and opened the door. The two girls walked down the aisle to the refrigerated case. While Kathy picked out their favorite sodas, Linda fished in her pocket for money.

They stopped in front of the check-out counter and handed the cashier the two sodas. Linda counted out the correct change.

Picking up the drinks, she turned to find Kathy huddled over the magazine rack.

"Ready to go?" Linda asked.

Kathy whipped around, an excited grin on her face. "Look at this," she said, waving a magazine in the air.

It was *Lookout,* one of their favorite magazines. On the cover was a picture of Cody, the hottest rock star around. Even Linda thought he was the greatest.

"What's it say?" she asked excitedly, peering over Kathy's shoulder.

"You won't believe it!" Kathy sounded as if she were about to scream. "It says Cody is living right here in Lockwood."

She looked up, a stunned expression on her face. "Linda, what if Cody is Jackie's mysterious father?"

8 ♦♦♦♦

"That's crazy." Linda grabbed the magazine from Kathy's hands and pored over the story.

Out loud, she read, " 'Seen driving from Lockwood's private airport in a white limousine was a tall, long-haired man with one earring. Who else could it be but the elusive Cody?' "

When she finished reading, Linda looked up at her friend. Kathy's eyes were wide, and her mouth was shaped in an O.

"A white limousine?" Linda repeated. "That does sound like the Lees."

"I know." Kathy glanced back at the story. "And it says that Cody was in Lockwood last Sunday." She paused, then said slowly, "That's the same day Jackie left the party early to pick up her father."

"In the white limousine," Linda finished.

Kathy closed the magazine. She set it back on the rack as if she were in a trance. "Linda, you don't really think . . ."

Linda nodded. "Could be. I knew something was going on. That would explain why those men were guarding the ranch. And that guy in the bushes could have been a reporter taking pictures."

"Cody—Jackie's father." Kathy shook her head. "It's hard to believe that a rock star could be somebody's father."

They walked from the drugstore.

"If he is her father, why wouldn't she tell us?" Kathy wondered.

Linda shrugged. "I don't know." She quickened her pace as they neared the Highway House, the restaurant that Kathy's parents owned. "Come on. I've got to call Bronco and ask him to pick me up, or Jackie will get to Rancho del Sol before I do."

"Well, I'm going to the ranch with you." Kathy started to hurry down the sidewalk. "I wouldn't miss this for the world."

"Hey, wait a minute." Linda had to jog to catch up with Kathy. "It's obvious Jackie doesn't want us to know."

Kathy stopped at the bottom of the Hamiltons' steps. "I promise I won't bring it up." Turning, she sprinted into the restaurant, calling over her shoulder, "But just wait till I tell Amy and Marni."

"You guys must have broken a speed record to get here," Linda said when Amy and Marni rode up Rancho del Sol's drive. The two girls halted their sweaty horses in front of the barn.

"Is Jackie here yet?" Amy asked, looking around excitedly.

"Did you ask her about Cody?" Marni chimed in.

"No, she's not here. And no, I didn't say anything to her," Linda said. "And don't you start, either. If Jackie wanted us to know Cody was her father, she would have told us."

"Where's Kathy?" Marni asked.

"Keeping watch like some kind of crazy groupie."

"Cody! Can you imagine?" Amy pretended to faint. "Just think—we know his daughter."

Linda rolled her eyes. "Why don't you put your horses in a stall?"

The two girls were dismounting when a shout made them look up.

Kathy came racing up the drive. "She's coming! She's coming!"

Kathy reached them just as the limo cruised past the house. Her face was bright red, and she was gasping for breath. Amy and Marni stared at the limo, their mouths hanging open.

Linda knew that no one would have to mention anything to Jackie. One glance at the girls' faces would tell her something was up.

Jackie swung the limo door open and bounced from the car. "Hi, guys," she greeted them.

Rushing toward her, Amy, Marni, and Kathy began talking at the same time. Quickly, Linda grabbed Jackie's elbow and steered her into the barn.

"They're here to watch your lesson," she said. "So let's show them how well you're doing."

As they walked down the aisle, Jackie looked back over her shoulder. The three other girls were chattering excitedly.

"What's going on?" she asked Linda. "They're acting so strange."

"They're always strange," Linda joked. "You just haven't been around them long enough."

They went into Copper's stall. Linda watched as Jackie bridled and saddled the horse.

"Great," Linda said. "Maybe tonight you'll be ready to canter."

She turned to open Copper's stall. Three faces were peering over the door.

"Well, well, must be the Three Stooges," Linda kidded.

"You did a nice job, tacking Copper up," Marni said, ignoring Linda's comment.

"Yeah," Amy agreed. "I bet your father will be proud of you."

Linda shot Amy a knock-it-off look. It didn't do any good.

"Will he be home this weekend?" Amy continued. "Or does his band have to pl— Ouch!"

Linda opened the stall so fast, the door caught Amy in the shins.

But it was too late. Jackie had heard her question.

"What do you mean, 'his band'?" she asked.

Kathy stepped forward. "Oh, come on, Jackie. You can tell us if Cody's your father. We think it's neat."

"I—uh—" Jackie stammered. With a confused frown, she looked back and forth among the four girls. Then, without another word, she picked up Copper's reins and pushed past Linda.

"Now you've done it," Marni said to her sister. "She'll never tell."

"Me? Kathy brought it up."

"Only after *you* blurted it out."

Linda started down the aisle after Jackie. She and Copper were in the middle of the ring. Linda watched as Jackie put her toe in the stirrup and started to mount. At the last minute, the saddle slipped sideways, but Jackie jumped back just in time.

Linda ran up to her. "That was lesson number twelve," she said with a smile. "Always Check Your Girth Before You Mount."

Jackie's face was hidden in Copper's mane, but Linda thought she heard a sigh.

"I think you mean lesson number three hundred and twelve," Jackie said grimly as she tightened the girth. "I feel like I'm starting all over again."

A commotion at the fence made them both look over. Yelling and pushing like little kids, Amy, Marni, and Kathy were climbing onto the top board trying to get the best seat.

"Look, you can't blame us," Linda said, hoping to explain her friends' behavior. "Cody's our favorite rock star."

"Mine, too," Jackie said, then slowly turned and led Copper over to the fence.

93

The three looked at her, their expressions apologetic.

"Hey, Jackie," Kathy finally said. "We didn't mean to embarrass you. But when we read in *Lookout* that Cody was living in Lockwood, Linda and I got this far-out idea that he was your father."

"He is."

"And then I called Amy and Marni and—" Kathy suddenly stopped talking. "He is!"

Amy and Marni screamed shrilly. Amy jumped up so high, she almost fell off the rail. Just in time, Marni caught her arm and pulled her up.

Even Linda was surprised. "He really is?" she asked.

"When can we meet him?" Kathy cried.

"Can I get his autograph?"

"What's it like having him around all the time?"

Suddenly, Jackie clapped her hands to her ears. "Stop!"

With startled expressions, the girls shut up.

"This is why I didn't tell you he was my father," Jackie said angrily. "I thought maybe you guys would be different. But you're just like everyone else. All of a sudden you want to be my best friend—just so you can meet Cody."

94

Abruptly, she spun around and mounted Copper. Linda put her hand on Copper's reins.

"That's not fair, Jackie," she said. "We were your friends before we found out about your dad."

"*You* were," Jackie said to Linda. Then her eyes flashed at the three sitting on the fence. "But no matter how hard I tried—"

"How hard *you* tried?" Kathy sputtered in protest. "When you first came, *I* was the one who tried to be nice. But you just stuck your nose up and didn't say a word—like you were too good for me."

"I did not."

"Yes, you did!" Marni agreed with Kathy. "You did it to me, too."

Jackie opened her mouth, ready to defend herself, then slowly shut it.

For a second, no one said anything. Kathy chewed on a fingernail. Linda smoothed Copper's mane. Jackie pretended to adjust her stirrup.

Finally, Linda cleared her throat. "Listen, Jackie. I understand why you kept your dad such a big secret. I probably would've done the same thing."

"Really?" Jackie looked surprised.

"Me, too," Kathy said. "It must be hard having screaming fans and nosy reporters hanging around all the time."

"It's terrible!" Jackie exclaimed. "And Dad's on the road so much, sometimes I think they see more of him than I do."

"I guess having a famous father might not be much fun," Amy said.

"Sometime's it's not. I mean, I'm really proud of him and all," Jackie added in a rush. "But I want to be liked for *me*. Not because I have a rock star for a father."

"I never thought of it that way," Marni said. "I remember how when I was class president, all these kids would buddy up to me just because they needed something."

"I guess we did act like that when we heard about your dad," Linda said.

"A little. But it sounds like I owe you guys an apology, too," Jackie said. "I guess I was so worried about not making friends that I wasn't a good friend in return."

"Yes, you were," Kathy protested. "You helped with my music and Amy and Marni's skit."

"And I had a good time giving you riding

lessons," Linda added. "Besides, if it wasn't for you, I'd be deaf by now."

"Deaf?" Jackie repeated, puzzled.

"Sure. Now that you're the lead singer for the Hombres, I don't have to listen to Larry's horrible yowling."

Everyone laughed, and Jackie started to smile—a big, happy smile, as if a giant weight had been lifted from her shoulders.

"Hey," Linda said. "Speaking of lessons, aren't you supposed to be having one?"

"Yeah," Kathy added. "We want to see what you've learned."

"Sounds good to me," Jackie said. She started to rein Copper into the middle of the ring, then stopped. "Hey, I've got a better idea. Since everyone has a horse here, why don't we go on a trail ride? This time, I promise I won't slow you down or be scared of anything."

9 ♦♦♦♦

"I vote we ride past the famous Mountain Lion Rock," Linda said fifteen minutes later as they rode from the ranch. She turned in the saddle to look at the line of riders behind her. "Even though it won't be as exciting without Bob and Larry's special effects."

"I second the motion," Jackie added with a grin. She and Copper were following right behind Amber.

Linda checked to see how Jackie was doing. Her friend sat tall yet relaxed on Copper. One hand held the reins lightly, the other stroked Copper's neck.

Linda could tell Jackie really enjoyed riding Copper. She knew her friend spent hours grooming and fussing over the mare.

Which makes her almost as bad as I am, Linda thought, reaching down to give Amber a pat. Then she signaled for everyone to jog. She knew their faster pace wouldn't give Jackie any trouble today.

Suddenly, a frightened cry came from behind her. Quickly, Linda turned in the saddle to see Copper prance sideways off the path. Jackie clutched the saddlehorn with both hands. The reins flapped uselessly on the mare's neck.

Linda opened her mouth to tell Copper to whoa, but a gasp came out instead. Jackie's horse was headed straight for a prairie dog hole!

"Watch out," Linda yelled. "There's a hole!"

Hearing the warning, Jackie sprang to life. Still holding onto the saddlehorn with one hand, she scooped up the reins with the other. She pulled Copper's head toward the path. At the same time, she dug her left heel into the mare's side.

Copper leapt back onto the path. Jackie flew up in the air, coming down on the saddle with a loud smack. But she didn't fall off.

Pulling herself upright, Jackie hollered a loud, "Whoa!"

Copper came to a standstill.

Linda steered Amber beside her friend. "Are you okay?"

Jackie's face was white as a ghost. But suddenly, she gave a loud whoop of laughter.

"No, I'm not okay. I'm *wonderful!*" Jackie gave everyone a huge grin. "I didn't panic or fall off or anything." Leaning over, she wrapped her arms around Copper's neck."

The other girls steered their horses in a circle around Copper.

"You were super," Kathy exclaimed. "For a second there, I thought you were going to fall."

"So did I." Jackie straightened in the saddle. "But then I remembered you telling me about the burrowing owl and its holes—how a horse could break a leg by falling into one. So I knew I had to do something before Copper got hurt."

"I wonder what made Copper jump off the path?" Linda wondered.

"Uh, I have a confession to make," Marni said. "It was my fault. I rode Midnight too close, and he tried to bite her. Sorry, Jackie."

"That's okay. It worked out fine. I proved to myself I can handle Copper. Now I know I'm ready to canter."

"Then let's get to it," Linda suggested. "Lesson number three hundred and thirteen." She pointed to a smooth, grassy stretch. "This will be the perfect spot."

"Are you sure there aren't any holes?" Jackie asked.

"Positive. And the ground's nice and soft," Linda added in a teasing voice. "Just in case somebody falls off."

On Saturday morning, the day of the talent show, Linda woke early. She felt as if she hadn't slept at all. And no wonder—she was so excited about the show, she'd tossed and turned all night.

She and Kelly had worked hard polishing their stunts, and tonight would be their chance to show them off. But it wasn't just the show. Linda was excited for Jackie, too.

For the last two weeks, Jackie had worked on cantering Copper, and she was doing very well. This morning, when Cody arrived from the airport, Jackie and Copper would be waiting at the end of the drive to greet him. Linda and Amber would be nearby—just in case.

As the limo entered Lucky Star Ranch, Jackie would trot alongside it. Linda felt sure Jackie's father would be so impressed with his daughter's riding that he'd buy her the horse she wanted so badly.

After a quick breakfast, Linda headed for the barn to groom Amber. When she walked past Copper's stall, she heard humming. She stopped and peered over the door. Jackie was already hard at work, brushing the mare.

"How'd you get here so early?" Linda asked.

"I had the chauffeur drop me off before he left for the airport." Jackie gave Copper's belly one last swipe, then stepped back to check her work. "I want Copper to shine like a new penny."

Linda smiled. "I asked Bronco if Copper was for sale. He said, 'Only to a girl who'll love her.' Sounds like he meant you."

"That would be great!" Jackie exclaimed. Then her voice grew solemn. "Now I just have to convince my dad."

Linda picked up a brush and opened Amber's stall door. "Your dad sounds a little tough on you."

"Yeah—but I understand. He's so worried about protecting me from reporters and crazy fans, he's gone a little overboard. You know, it's like he wants me to have a normal life, but he's been a star for so long, he's not quite sure what normal is."

"Then let's show him what *normal* kids do in

Lockwood," Linda said. "We ride everywhere on horseback."

"All right!"

Half an hour later, the two horses were tacked up for the ride to Lucky Star Ranch. Copper wore Amber's fancy show saddle and bridle. Jackie had even bought leather chaps. She zipped them over her jeans, then put on the cowboy hat Linda had lent her.

"Your dad won't recognize you," Linda said as she mounted.

They took their time riding to the ranch. On a safe stretch of field, Jackie practiced cantering Copper. By the time they reached the fence separating the two ranches, Jackie was smiling confidently.

"Just remember, if Copper starts going too fast, pull back on the reins and tell her whoa," Linda said.

Jackie nodded, but Linda could tell her mind was elsewhere. Jackie was staring toward the ranch house, a frown on her face.

"I can't believe it!" she cried in dismay. "The place is swarming with reporters—that ruins everything."

Linda stood up in the stirrups to get a better

view. A dozen cars and vans were parked in front of Lucky Star's gates.

"You can still do it," she told Jackie. "You'll just have to meet your dad before he gets to the crowd."

"You're right." Jackie brightened. "But he won't get to see me ride for a very long time."

"Better that than not at all."

Jackie agreed, and they rode across the pasture toward the milling people. Linda couldn't believe how many fans were there. No wonder Cody had tried to keep the ranch a secret.

Luckily, the crowd of reporters gave them only a quick glance, and no one else paid any attention to the girls. They probably think we're just two nosy fans, Linda thought.

As they rode past a van, Linda patted Amber. The mare nervously flicked her ears at the strange goings-on. Linda glanced over her shoulder at Jackie. Fortunately, Copper was plodding along quietly.

The girls were nearing the main gate when someone shouted Cody's name. Several reporters began to run down the drive. Linda twisted in the saddle to see better. The limo was coming.

Before Linda could say anything, Jackie kicked Copper into a trot, heading down the drive toward the limo. Reporters were running to and fro, bumping into one another like a herd of cattle about to stampede.

Linda reined Amber away from the crowd. Over the top of a van, she spied Copper. Jackie was dogging the mare right toward her dad's limo. Linda craned her neck, trying to see if the two were okay, but there was so much dust and confusion, she couldn't tell.

Then a man waved his arms in the air and pointed at Jackie. "That's Cody's daughter," he yelled.

Startled, Linda watched as the news people became even more excited. Two men jumped into a van and floored it. They sped down the road after Jackie. One man leaned out the window, his video camera running.

Amber snorted and pranced sideways. As the limousine drew closer, Linda caught sight of Jackie. She and Copper were cantering next to her father's car. A triumphant look was on Jackie's face as she waved to her father inside the limo.

The van circled around them. Then, gunning the motor, the driver pulled alongside Copper so the mare was sandwiched between the van and the limousine.

The man with the camera began shouting to Jackie. Copper flattened her ears and ducked away from him, almost running into the limo. Linda could tell the mare was becoming frightened.

"Come on, Amber," Linda whispered. Weaving through the crowd, she reined her horse toward the driveway.

She had to help Jackie, but the shouting people were making Amber as nervous as Copper, and the speeding van was blocking the way.

The limo slowed to a stop. Trying to escape the clattering van, Jackie jerked Copper's rein, turning the mare away from the noisy vehicle. Copper broke into a gallop.

Why didn't the van stop? Linda wondered. Anyone could see it was scaring the horse.

She urged Amber into a canter. If she could swing in front of Copper, maybe she could slow the horse down.

Then, with a startled cry, Linda realized where Jackie and Copper were headed. Ahead of them was the old orchard—and the hidden barbed wire fence!

Linda slackened the reins and kicked Amber. Like a flash of golden light, the palomino flew toward Copper.

"Jackie!" Linda yelled, but the wind blew her cry of warning into the air.

Jackie would never hear her in time. And the fence was so overgrown with weeds, she'd never see it. Linda leaned low on Amber's neck. Jackie and Copper were about fifty feet away. They had to catch them before they hit the fence. "Go, girl, go!" Linda whispered into Amber's ears. Amber flicked them once, then her powerful stride began to eat up the ground between the two horses.

They were going to make it. Ten feet behind Copper, Linda again cried out a warning. But Jackie still couldn't hear. Linda could tell that Copper was confused and frightened. Jackie shouted for Copper to stop, but the shouts only made the horse run faster.

Linda steered Amber as close to Copper as she could. Then she squeezed her legs against the palomino's side. With one last burst of speed, Amber pulled alongside Copper.

Linda reached for the other horse's reins, but

Copper shied as soon as she saw Linda's arm. Jackie shot her a pleading look.

How was she going to stop her?

"Easy, girl." Linda steadied Amber next to Copper. When the two horses were neck and neck, she took a deep breath and jumped.

10 ♦♦♦♦

It wasn't until she landed with a thud on Copper's broad rump that Linda realized she had her eyes shut tight. Gasping with relief, she wrapped her arms around Jackie's waist.

"Jackie," she cried in her friend's ear. "We've got to calm Copper—there's a barbed-wire fence ahead."

Jackie sat back farther in the saddle and pulled even harder on the reins. At the same time, Linda called soothingly to the frightened mare.

Together they got the mare to slow to a trot.

"Whoa," Jackie said in a calm voice, and this time, the mare skidded to a stop.

Puffing and sweaty, her sides heaving, Copper halted ten feet in front of the deadly barbed wire.

Linda could feel her own hands trembling. In front of her, Jackie was gasping for breath.

Amber! Quickly, Linda looked around. What if Amber ran into the fence?

But Amber was standing under a pear tree, munching on fruit as if she hadn't a care in the world.

Linda burst out laughing as she slid off Copper's rear. Jackie began to laugh with her.

"You pick the craziest times to crack up," Jackie said, gasping for air.

"I can't help it. I'm just so happy everything turned out okay."

Jackie nodded. "Me, too. And thanks! I had no idea about that barbed wire."

The limousine pulled up behind them. Before it had a chance to stop, a tall, long-haired man opened the door and sprang from the back-seat.

Linda recognized him immediately. Cody! Several stern-faced men hurried from the car to surround him protectively.

"Jackie, are you okay?" Cody grabbed his daughter around the waist and pulled her off Copper. "I was terrified!" He hugged her against him.

"Dad," Jackie protested, pulling away. "I'm fine."

"Thank goodness. I didn't know what to think when that crazy horse galloped away. What kind of a stunt was that? You could've killed yourself."

"It wasn't a stunt. I was trying to get away from the reporters, and—"

Without letting her finish, Cody took Jackie by the elbow. "Quick, into the car before we get mobbed."

"But what about Copper?" Jackie cried.

"Do you think I'd let you on that horse again?" Cody frowned. "Your friend can take that animal away—and lock her in a stall where she belongs."

"But she's the horse I want to buy. That's why I rode her over here."

"We'll discuss this later." With a firm grip on his daughter's arm, Cody steered Jackie toward the limousine. Linda caught up Copper's reins and watched as the limo backed away.

Jackie's dad was really angry. As the limo roared away in a cloud of dust, Linda wondered if Cody would ever let Jackie ride Copper again.

* * *

"How did it go at the Lees'?" Bronco and Doña greeted Linda as she rode Amber up to the barn. Wearily, she tossed Copper's reins to Bronco.

"Don't ask," Linda groaned, sliding from the saddle like a sack of potatoes.

Doña looked puzzled. "As hard as you girls worked, it couldn't have gone that badly."

"Let's just say a mob of reporters spoiled everything."

"Reporters?" Bronco looked puzzled.

"Yeah, they were there because of Cody."

"Who's Cody?" Bronco asked, even more puzzled.

"A world-famous rock star, dear," Doña told her husband. Then she patted Linda's shoulder. "I'm sorry. How did the reporters find the ranch so quickly?"

"There was an article in one of the fan magazines," Linda explained as they led the horses into the barn. "Remember when I told you about that guy taking my picture? I bet he was spying on the ranch."

She opened the stall door for Amber and began unsaddling her. The palomino's back and neck were streaked with dried dust. She'd definitely need a good bath before— Oh, no, the talent show! In the excitement, Linda had forgotten all about it. She hoped Cody would let Jackie appear.

"I'm not surprised," Bronco called from Copper's stall. "Reporters are like bloodhounds."

"Can you help me with Copper?" Linda called back. "I've got tons to do before tonight."

"That reminds me, young lady," Bronco said. "I hope you and your friend Kelly know what you're doing."

Linda hid a smile. Her grandfather sounded just like Jackie's dad. "Don't worry. I've had plenty of practice."

A car pulled up outside the barn. "It's the Lees' limousine," Doña called.

Linda peered over the stall door. She could see Jackie and her father getting out of the car.

Linda noticed how serious they both looked as they walked down the aisle.

"Copper!" Jackie exclaimed, crossing over to the mare's stall. "Are you all right?"

Bronco stepped into the aisle and held out his hand. "Hello, Mr. Lee," he said. "Welcome to Rancho del Sol."

"Please, call me Harry," Cody said, shaking hands with Bronco, then Doña.

113

Harry? Linda almost laughed. The famous rock star was actually named Harry.

Harry Lee, alias Cody, turned to watch Jackie busily unsaddling Copper.

"It appears your daughter's caught the horse bug," Doña said with a laugh.

Cody nodded. "And not just any horse, she tells me. It has to be this one. But I don't know. It seems to me that riding a big animal like that is about as safe as driving a car without brakes."

Bronco nodded seriously. "Maybe if I tell you how safe riding is, you might change your mind," he said. "Though I'd be lying if I said accidents never happen. But your daughter's been getting lessons from the best." He winked at Linda. "And Copper's as quiet and well trained as any horse."

"I find that hard to believe after what I saw this morning," Cody said doubtfully. He gave Jackie a worried look.

"Just what *did* happen?" Doña asked.

With a rush of words, Linda and Jackie explained everything. Bronco's brows rose when Linda told how she'd jumped onto Copper's back. He opened his mouth as if to say something about that, but Doña quietly took his arm and gave it a squeeze.

Linda flashed her grandmother a smile of thanks.

"Well . . ." Bronco drawled when they were through with the wild tale. "I'd say it wasn't the girls' or the horses' fault. I'd say you need to take down that old barbed wire."

"Maybe you're right." Cody turned and stared at Copper over the stall door. "I know my daughter thinks so. We had a long talk. Jackie tells me I'm too strict and overprotective. And I guess I have to agree with her."

He faced the others. "All I want is for her life to be normal. So if normal in Lockwood is having your own horse, then"—he finally smiled—"I guess Jackie needs her own horse."

"Oh, Dad!" Jackie threw her arms around his neck.

"But only if Linda keeps giving you lessons," he added in a stern voice.

"It's a deal," Jackie said happily. "That is, if it's okay, with you, Linda," she quickly added.

"It's more than okay—it's great."

"Well, Cody, I mean, Harry," Doña said with a laugh, "now that it's all settled, how'd you like to come into the house for a cold drink?"

"I'd love to," he replied.

Linda watched the grown-ups walk to the door. She could hardly believe it—the greatest rock star ever, standing right here in her barn.

In the middle of the fairground arena, Amy and Marni were just finishing their pantomime for the talent show. Linda, holding Amber's reins, waited outside the arena gate. She could barely see the girls over the crowd, but from the sound of clapping, the sisters' mirror act was a hit.

Fortunately, she'd been sitting in the grandstand when Kathy had performed. Her gymnastics routine had been flawless, and Linda had stood with the rest of the crowd to applaud her.

Now it was Linda's turn.

She searched for Kelly. The older girl was already on Cinder, calmly talking with one of her friends. Linda waved frantically to catch Kelly's attention.

"Relax," Kelly said with a laugh. "You'll—"

Kelly didn't get a chance to finish. Amy and Marni bounced jubilantly from the ring, shouting, "You guys are next."

Linda quickly mounted and after patting Amber for good luck, followed Kelly into the arena. Lights beamed from all sides, making it hard to see the audience. But Linda knew that hundreds of people were out there.

The horses broke into a canter, and she and Kelly circled the arena once. In the middle of the oval area was a short wooden platform used as a stage for some of the acts.

Over the loudspeaker, music began to play. That was the signal to begin.

Side by side the two horses cantered in perfect harmony. At each end of the ring, they looped together in a perfect figure eight, then they split up, circled, and met once again.

The audience clapped. Linda knew how beautiful pure black Cinder and golden Amber looked side by side. When they moved in synch with the music, she could imagine they were really a sight to behold.

Then the beat of the music grew faster, which was Kelly's cue to begin her stunt. The older girl cantered her bareback horse around the platform, cutting close as if it were a barrel in a barrel race. Then she swung her leg over Cinder's back and dismounted on top of the platform.

She took a few running steps to regain her

balance. Then, as Cinder cantered to the other side, she raced across the platform and leapt back onto her horse.

The crowd roared.

Linda clapped with them, then took a deep breath. It was her turn.

The music quickened again. Linda signaled to Amber to canter. At the end of the arena, they met Kelly and Cinder, and the two horses headed down the side of the arena at a gallop.

Neck and neck they raced, so close together that Linda's stirrup touched Cinder's side. When their strides were perfectly in step, Linda knew it was the right time to jump.

Just as she made her leap, Cinder veered sideways. Like a shadow, Amber swerved with her.

With a startled cry, Linda landed on Cinder's back. She grabbed Kelly and pulled herself upright. Then she quickly waved her hand in the air and smiled at the audience. Maybe they'd think the slip-up was all part of the act.

As the audience applauded, the two horses galloped toward the platform. Linda could hear a gasp as Cinder and Amber leapt onto it and slid to a halt. The two girls raised their cowboy hats in the air. Then the horses jumped from the platform and cantered out of the arena.

"You were fantastic," Doña exclaimed when she and Bronco met Linda outside the arena.

"Fantastic," Bronco said. "You two were wonderful. But if I'd had any idea that's what you were practicing, I'm not sure I would have allowed it."

"Well, I told Linda she could," Doña said to her husband. "And I knew Amber could do it."

Jackie rushed up, carrying a guitar.

"You and Kelly were super-terrific," she said. "I think I'll learn that trick next."

"Oh, no you don't!" a voice said behind her. Cody strode up next to his daughter. He was disguised in dark glasses and a cowboy hat. On his shoulder, a guitar hung from a strap.

"Just kidding, Dad. You know I'd rather sing duets." She smiled proudly at Linda and her grandparents. "Guess what? Dad's going to sing a song with the band, then do an act with me."

"That's really neat," Linda said. Already, she could hear the Hombres tuning up on the stage.

"Ladies and gentlemen, may I have your attention," the announcer blasted over the loudspeakers. "We have a special surprise for you. We present

Jackie Lee and the Hombres and with them, another Lockwood star, the one and only CODY!''

The band broke into a rousing rock tune. Waving their hands at the audience, Jackie and her father ran across the arena. The crowd went wild.

Linda led Amber to the railing so she could see better. For a second, she laid her hand on Amber's neck.

"I didn't get a chance to thank you," she whispered. "If it wasn't for you and your quick thinking, the stunt would have been ruined."

Onstage, Jackie sang as if everyone in Lockwood were a special friend. Linda smiled as she stroked Amber's soft nose. She didn't think Jackie would be lonely in her new home anymore.

The music grew louder and the audience roared. Jackie and her father began a duet, and they were fantastic.

In fact, they were so terrific, Linda thought, they even made Bob and Larry sound good.

She grinned to herself.

Well, *almost.*